# DRACULA

*Bram Stoker's*

# DRACULA

RE-EDITED BY *Jan Needle*

ILLUSTRATED BY

*Gary Blythe*

WALKER BOOKS
AND SUBSIDIARIES
LONDON · BOSTON · SYDNEY · AUCKLAND

# CONTENTS

## Book Three – The Evil Spreads

## Book Four – The Passion of Mina Harker

## Book Five – The Jaws of Hell

*FOR KIRI*
*Not a Bride of Dracula, but a Groom.*
*And a Power in the land.*
*J. N.*


*FOR LIN*
*G. B.*

# "We Shall Wake to Sanity"

## A 21ST-CENTURY NOTE

The story of Count Dracula is, not to put too fine a point on it, the stuff of nightmares. Much of it takes place in a madhouse, and many of the participants are insane – or fear almost constantly that the events they are involved in must surely drive them mad. Bram Stoker, though, the man who organized the evidence, was prepared, at last, to present it all as "simple fact".

When he began to gather raw material, it existed as a huge unsorted mass. There were hundreds of pages of typed notes, and others in longhand and in shorthand. There were phonograph cylinders, newspaper cuttings, bills and letterheads of companies, the scribblings of semi-literate drunkards – for an editor, a truly daunting task. Stoker, who started work in 1890, waited seven years before he felt he was ready to go before the public with it – and recognized even then that it was "a history almost at variance with the possibilities of latter-day belief."

That, to some, may seem an understatement. It is a story told by several different people, all with different views, opinions, certainties. The dates, times and places Stoker left to us are sometimes jumbled, odd and unreliable, and the settings are appalling and bizarre – a madhouse, a bleak and awful castle, an ancient cemetery. The central character is said by Stoker to be many hundred years old, but he bursts with a hideous vitality which he renews and fires up by drinking human blood.

Even some of the people who suffer and interpret the events seem sometimes not so sure that their story is all fact. Dr John (Jack) Seward, in whose lunatic asylum much of the action takes place, wonders at one point if "my long habit of life amongst the insane is beginning to tell upon my own brain", and later confides in his diary, "I sometimes think we must be all mad and that we shall wake to sanity in strait-waistcoats."

And by the end of it, those who survive are confident – deluded? – enough to honestly believe that they, and they alone, have saved the world...

These people, when they first get drawn into the awful mystery, are in many ways a strange and problematic group. They are young – aged from eighteen to a few years upwards – and range from an earnest (and at first quite dull) solicitor's clerk, Jonathan Harker, to a wealthy English aristocrat, Arthur Holmwood. Jonathan Harker has an adoring fiancée, Mina Murray, whose greatest ambition, apparently, is to become a good wife and a selfless helpmate. Meanwhile her best friend, Lucy Westenra, is a most outrageous flirt who is being courted by three men simultaneously – all of whom propose to her on the same day!

Her suitors, naturally, behave like perfect gentlemen, but Lucy – gorgeous, vivacious, giddy – inevitably becomes the first to fall for Count Dracula's more brutal and effective seduction techniques. Which means that all three have to save her – with injections of their precious life – and all three are somehow jealous of the others because they've done so.

One of the suitors, Dr Seward, is a strange man; but he has stranger inmates in his private mental home. Most interesting is a morose and dangerous character introduced in Seward's diary as "R. M. Renfield, aged 59" – who eats flies voraciously, and wishes to graduate to bigger animals while awaiting the arrival of his mysterious "master", revealed at last to be Count Dracula. And Seward has a master, too – Professor Van Helsing, who is called upon to save them all when Lucy Westenra offers up her naked neck to her demon lover's fangs.

Van Helsing, a Dutchman, was Seward's tutor once, and loves him like a son. Very quickly he loves Lucy also, then Mina, who is now Mrs Harker. He alone knows the nature of the all-pervading evil they are faced with, although he is very loath to spell it out. How vampires can be centuries old, can live for ever and can infect anyone whose blood they suck with their own eternal curse. How victims become "Un-Dead", afraid of daylight, terrified of God, but destined to roam by night seeking new throats to pierce and drain. How death – and peace – for these foul, *tragic creatures can be brought only through most ruthless savagery, like cutting heads off beautiful young women and driving wooden stakes into their defenceless breasts.*

*Dr Seward, whose life and expertise is lunatics, remember, at one stage wonders if this great old man has been driven crazy by the horrors he has seen. And then he wonders if Van Helsing could have somehow done it all himself. All the blood, all the cruelty, all the madness: perhaps it is the sickest fantasy of one diseased and tortured brain. Swamped by the sea of words, images, bizarre unpleasant happenings, it is difficult to keep a grip on reality, to sort out facts from awful, chilling fantasy.*

*Bram Stoker, as far as history tells us, did keep a grip; he was not driven mad by working through this mass of documents to piece together the story. Your present editor, also, feels fairly sure that he is likewise sane – at least, as sane as when he set out on the giant task. For yourselves, read it, and wonder. Or better, maybe – read it, and* hope.

*Jan Needle*

*Book One*

THE BRINGING
*of the* PLAGUE

# 1

# The Crucifix

Jonathan Harker, young, naïve and hopeful, set off from England to complete the sale of a country house at Purfleet, near the edge of London, to a count who lived in the heart of Central Europe, Transylvania. Although young, Jonathan was ambitious, and on the first rung of the ladder to success. His employer, Mr Peter Hawkins, of Exeter, was more like a father to him than a boss, and had entrusted him with this most important task because of his own illness.

Jonathan's intention was to complete the business as quickly as ever he could, return to England and marry his fiancée, Mina (Wilhelmina) Murray, a school assistant who was planning to become his unofficial secretary. Even given that the journey involved travel by train, ferry and stagecoach, he was hoping to be abroad for only two weeks or so. He was sadly, sadly wrong.

Leaving London at the end of April, he kept a journal of his travellings, in shorthand so that he could share it with Mina, who had become an expert too. The first entry is dated 3 May, *by which time he had reached Bistritz, in modern-day Romania, from where he could travel onward only by horse-drawn coach (the "diligence").*

*Jonathan had already noticed the extreme difference between the western world he was leaving when he crossed the Danube at Buda-Pesth, and the (to him) new lands of the east. A howling dog underneath his hotel window had given him a bad night's sleep, and he had had "all sorts of queer dreams." The next day, as his unpunctual train dawdled through the countryside, he commented on the "picturesqueness" of many of the peasants: "The strangest figures were the Slovaks, who are more barbarian than the rest, with their big cowboy hats, great baggy dirty-white trousers, white linen shirts and enormous heavy leather belts, nearly a foot wide, all studded over with brass nails. They wore high boots, with their trousers tucked into them, and had long black hair and heavy black moustaches. On the stage they would be set down at once as some old Oriental band of brigands."*

*When he reached the frontier town, however, and found his way to the Golden Krone Hotel, to which Count Dracula had directed him in his letters to England, things got better. The hotel was old-fashioned, which filled him with delight, and he was greeted by a cheerful old woman and her husband, who could understand his "smattering of German" quite adequately. The old man, indeed, handed him a letter, which turned out to be from his host.*

*         ★      ★      ★*

My Friend,

Welcome to the Carpathians. I am anxiously expecting you. Sleep well tonight. At three tomorrow the diligence will start for Bukovina: a place on it is kept for you. At the Borgo Pass my carriage will await you and will bring you to me. I trust that your journey from London has been a happy one, and that you will enjoy your stay in my beautiful land.

Your friend,

DRACULA

*By morning, though, some things had changed. The couple had also had instructions from the count and, when Jonathan tried to question them about the castle he was going to, seemed fearful, and crossed themselves. Later, just before he left to catch the coach, the old lady came to his room, almost hysterical.*

*"Must you go?" she pleaded with him. "Oh, young Herr, must you go?"*

*Jonathan's journal continued:* She was in such an excited state that she seemed to have lost her grip of what German she knew, and mixed it all up with some other language which I did not know at all. When I told her that I must go at once, and that I was engaged on important business, she asked, "Do you know where you are going?"

She was in such evident distress that I tried to comfort her, but without effect. Finally she went down on her knees and implored me. It was all very ridiculous, but there was business to be done, and I could allow nothing to interfere with it. I therefore tried to raise her up, and said, as gravely as I could, that I thanked her, but my duty was imperative. She then rose and dried her eyes, and taking a crucifix from her neck, offered it to me.

I did not know what to do, for, as an English Churchman, I have been taught to regard such things as in some measure idolatrous, and yet it seemed so ungracious to refuse an old lady meaning so well and in such a state of mind.

She saw, I suppose, the doubt in my face, for she put the rosary round my neck and said, "For your mother's sake," and went out of the room. I am writing up this part of the diary whilst I am waiting for the coach, which is, of course, late; and the crucifix is still round my neck.

Whether it is the old lady's fear, or the many ghostly traditions of this place, or the crucifix itself, I do not know, but I am not feeling nearly as easy in my mind as usual.

If this book should ever reach Mina before I do, let it bring my goodbye. Here comes the coach!

# 2

# The Children of the Night

The journey, in a carriage drawn at breakneck speed by four horses harnessed side by side, was bad enough, to be sure. But there seemed to be something else bothering the other passengers – and the driver. Before they started, Jonathan noticed a crowd staring at him, using words which he looked up in a dictionary: "Ordog" – Satan, "pokol" – hell, "stregoica" – witch, and "vrolok" and "vlkoslak" – werewolf, or vampire.

He also noticed them making a gesture – the sign of the cross and two fingers pointed towards him – which a fellow passenger told him reluctantly was to guard against the evil eye. This, Jonathan noted dryly, "was not very pleasant" for him, "just starting for an unknown place to meet an unknown man."

On the way, for some obscure reason the driver seemed prepared to flog his horses almost to their deaths. And when they reached the Borgo Pass at least an hour before the coach was scheduled to, the passengers all let out "a sigh of gladness" and the driver told the Englishman ("in German worse than my *own") that he had obviously not been expected after all, the rendezvous was clearly a misunderstanding, and he should continue with them on to Bukovina.*

*At which point the peasants screamed and crossed themselves as a four-horse calash appeared at great speed as if from nowhere, overtook them and clattered to a halt.*

*Jonathan wrote:* I could see from the flash of our lamps that the horses were coal-black and splendid animals. They were driven by a tall man, with a long brown beard and a great black hat, which seemed to hide his face from us. I could only see the gleam of a pair of very bright eyes, which seemed red in the lamplight, as he turned.

. The lamplight fell on a hard-looking mouth, with very red lips and sharp-looking teeth, as white as ivory. One of my companions whispered to another, "Denn die Todten reiten schnell." ("For the dead travel fast.") The strange driver evidently heard the words, for he looked up with a gleaming smile.

*This man, who helped Jonathan into the new carriage with a "grip of steel", took him on a long, wild journey that he remembered only as a jumbled nightmare. It involved howling dogs, driving snow, strange blue flickering lights and a quantity of wolves, "with white teeth and lolling red tongues, with long, sinewy limbs and shaggy hair." Strangest of all, the driver could control them, merely with a gesture of his arms.*

*Then suddenly, after an interminable climb, they were pulling into the courtyard of "a vast ruined castle, from whose* tall black windows came no ray of light, and whose broken battlements showed a jagged line against the moonlit sky."

The driver, with massive strength, lifted Jonathan and his baggage down, then drove off, leaving him all alone. The journal records his great discomfort, and the black and eerie scene.

## Jonathan Harker's Journal

5 May – I stood in silence where I was, for I did not know what to do. Of bell or knocker there was no sign. Through these frowning walls and dark window openings it was not likely that my voice could penetrate.

The time I waited seemed endless, and I felt doubts and fears crowding upon me. What sort of place had I come to, and among what kind of people? What sort of grim adventure was it on which I had embarked? Was this a customary incident in the life of a solicitor's clerk sent out to explain the purchase of a London estate to a foreigner?

Solicitor's clerk! Mina would not like that. Solicitor – for just before leaving London I got word that my examination was successful; and I am now a full-blown solicitor! I began to rub my eyes and pinch myself to see if I were awake. It all seemed like a horrible nightmare to me, and I expected that I should suddenly awake, and find myself at home, with the dawn struggling in through the windows, as I had now and again felt in the morning after a day of overwork.

But my flesh answered the pinching test, and my eyes were not to be deceived. I was indeed awake and among the Carpathians. All I could do now was to be patient, and to wait the coming of morning.

Just as I had come to this conclusion I heard a heavy step approaching behind the great door, and saw through the chinks the gleam of a coming light. Then there was the sound of rattling chains and the clanking of massive bolts drawn back. A key was turned with the loud grating noise of long disuse, and the great door swung back.

Within stood a tall old man, clean-shaven save for a long white moustache, and clad in black from head to foot, with-

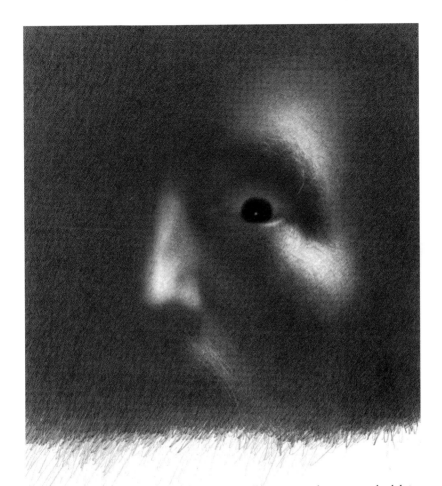

out a single speck of colour about him anywhere. He held in his hand an antique silver lamp, in which the flame burned without a chimney or globe of any kind, throwing long quivering shadows as it flickered in the draught of the open door. The old man motioned me in with his right hand with a courtly gesture, saying in excellent English, but with a strange intonation: "Welcome to my house! Enter freely and of your own free will!"

He made no motion of stepping to meet me, but stood like a statue, as though his gesture of welcome had fixed him into stone. The instant, however, that I had stepped over the threshold, he moved impulsively forward, and holding out his hand grasped mine with a strength which made me wince, an effect which was not lessened by the fact that it seemed as cold as ice – more like the hand of a dead than a living man.

"Count Dracula?"

He bowed in a courtly way as he replied, "I am Dracula, and I bid you welcome, Mr Harker, to my house. Come in; the night air is chill, and you must need to eat and rest."

He insisted on carrying my traps along the passage, and then up a great winding stair, and along another great passage, on whose stone floor our steps rang heavily. At the end of this he threw open a heavy door, and I rejoiced to see within a well-lit room in which a table was spread for supper, and on whose mighty hearth a great fire of logs flamed and flared.

The Count himself came forward and took off the cover of a dish, and I fell to at once on an excellent roast chicken. This, with some cheese and a salad and a bottle of old Tokay, of which I had two glasses, was my supper. During the time I was eating it the Count asked me many questions as to my journey, and I told him by degrees all I had experienced.

By this time I had finished, and by my host's desire had

drawn up a chair by the fire and begun to smoke a cigar which he offered me, at the same time excusing himself that he did not smoke. I had now an opportunity of observing him, and found him of a very marked physiognomy.

His face was a strong – a very strong – aquiline, with high bridge of the thin nose and peculiarly arched nostrils; with lofty domed forehead, and hair growing scantily round the temples, but profusely elsewhere. His eyebrows were very massive, almost meeting over the nose, and with bushy hair that seemed to curl in its own profusion.

The mouth, so far as I could see it under the heavy moustache, was fixed and rather cruel-looking, with peculiarly sharp white teeth; these protruded over the lips, whose remarkable ruddiness showed astonishing vitality in a man of his years.

For the rest, his ears were pale, and at the tops extremely pointed; the chin was broad and strong, and the cheeks firm though thin. The general effect was one of extraordinary pallor.

Hitherto I had noticed the backs of his hands as they lay on his knees in the firelight, and they had seemed rather white and fine; but seeing them now close to me, I could not but notice that they were rather coarse – broad, with squat fingers. Strange to say, there were hairs in the centre of the palm. The nails were long and fine, and cut to a sharp point.

As the Count leaned over me and his hands touched me, I could not repress a shudder. It may have been that his breath was rank, but a horrible feeling of nausea came over me, which, do what I would, I could not conceal. The Count, evidently noticing it, drew back; and with a grim sort of smile, which showed more than he had yet done his protuberant teeth, sat himself down again on his own side of the fireplace.

We were both silent for a while, and as I looked towards the window I saw the first dim streak of the coming dawn. There seemed a strange stillness over everything; but as I listened I heard, as if from down below in the valley, the howling of many wolves. The Count's eyes gleamed, and he said, "Listen to them – the children of the night. What music they make!"

Seeing, I suppose, some expression in my face strange to him, he added, "Ah, sir, you dwellers in the city cannot enter into the feelings of the hunter." Then he rose and said, "But you must be tired. Your bedroom is all ready, and tomorrow you shall sleep as late as you will. I have to be away till the afternoon; so sleep well and dream well!" And, with a courteous bow, he opened for me himself the door to the octagonal room, and I entered my bedroom...

I am all in a sea of wonders. I doubt; I fear; I think strange things which I dare not confess to my own soul. God keep me, if only for the sake of those dear to me!

# 3

# A Prisoner in Hell

## Jonathan Harker's Journal

*7 May* – It is again early morning, but I have rested and enjoyed the last twenty-four hours. I slept till late in the day, and awoke of my own accord. When I had dressed myself I went into the room where we had supped, and found a cold breakfast laid out, with coffee kept hot by the pot being placed on the hearth. There was a card on the table, on which was written: "I have to be absent for a while. Do not wait for me – D." So I set to and enjoyed a hearty meal.

When I had done, I looked for a bell, so that I might let the servants know I had finished, but I could not find one. There are certainly odd deficiencies in the house, considering the extraordinary evidences of wealth which are round me. The table service is of gold, and so beautifully wrought that it must be of immense value. The curtains and upholstery of the chairs and sofas and the hangings of my bed are of the costliest and most beautiful fabrics, and must have been of fabulous value when they were made, for they are centuries old, though in excellent order.

But still in none of the rooms is there a mirror. There is not even a toilet glass on my table, and I had to get the little shaving glass from my bag before I could either shave or brush my hair. I have not yet seen a servant anywhere, or heard a sound near the castle except the howling of wolves.

When I had finished my meal, I looked about for something to read, for I did not like to go about the castle until I had asked the Count's permission. There was absolutely nothing in the room, book, newspaper, or even writing materials; so I opened another door in the room and found a sort of library. The door opposite mine I tried, but found it locked.

Whilst I was looking at the books, the door opened, and the Count entered. He saluted me in a hearty way, and hoped that I had had a good night's rest. Then he went on, "I am glad you found your way in here, for I am sure there is much that will interest you. These companions" – and he laid his hand on some of the books – "have been good friends to me, and for some years past, ever since I had the idea of going to London, have given me many, many hours of pleasure. Through them I have come to know your great England; and to know her is to love her. I long to go through the crowded streets of your mighty London, to be in the midst of the whirl and rush of humanity, to share its life, its change, its death.

"But alas! As yet I only know your tongue through books.

To you, my friend, I look that I know it to speak."

"But, Count," I said, "you know and speak English thoroughly!" He bowed gravely.

"Not so," he answered. "Well I know that, did I move and speak in your London, none there are who would not know me for a stranger. That is not enough for me. Here I am noble; I am *boyar*; the common people know me, and I am master. But a stranger in a strange land, he is no one; I have been so long master that I would be master still. You shall, I trust, rest here with me a while, so that by our talking I may learn the English intonation."

Of course I said all I could about being willing, and asked if I might come into that room when I chose. He answered, "Yes, certainly," and added, "You may go anywhere you wish in the castle, except where the doors are locked, where of course you will not wish to go. There is reason that all things are as they are, and did you see with my eyes and know with my knowledge, you would perhaps better understand. We are in Transylvania; and Transylvania is not England. Our ways are not your ways, and there shall be to you many strange things. Come, tell me of London and of the house which you have procured for me."

With an apology for my remissness, I went into my own room to get the papers from my bag. Whilst I was placing them in order I heard a rattling of china and silver in the next room, and as I passed through, noticed that the table had been cleared and the lamp lit, for it was by this time deep into the dark.

We went thoroughly into the business of the purchase of the estate at Purfleet. When I had told him the facts and got his signature to the necessary papers, and had written a letter with them ready to post to Mr Hawkins, he began to ask me how I had come across so suitable a place. I read to him the notes which I had made at the time, and which I inscribe here:

"At Purfleet, on a by-road, I came across just such a place as seemed to be required, and where was displayed a dilapidated notice that the place was for sale. It was surrounded by a high wall, of ancient structure, built of heavy stones, and has not been repaired for a large number of years. The closed gates were of heavy old oak and iron, all eaten with rust.

"The estate is called Carfax. There are many trees on it, which make it in places gloomy, and there is a deep, dark-looking pond or small lake, evidently fed by some springs, as the water is clear and flows away in a fair-sized stream. The house is very large and is close to an old chapel or church. I could not enter it, as I had not the key of the door leading to it from the house, but I have taken with my Kodak views of it from various points. There are but few houses close at hand, one being a very large house only recently added to and formed into a private lunatic asylum. It is not, however, visible from the grounds."

When I had finished, he said, "I am glad that it is old and big. I myself am of an old family, and to live in a new house would kill me.

"A house cannot be made habitable in a day; and, after all,

how few days go to make up a century. I rejoice also that there is a chapel of old times. We Transylvanian nobles love not to think that our bones may be amongst the common dead."

Presently, with an excuse, he left me, asking me to put all my papers together. He was some little time away, and I began to look at some of the books around me. One was an atlas, which I found opened naturally at England, as if that map had been much used. On looking at it I found in certain places little rings marked, and on examining these I noticed that one was near London on the east side, manifestly where his new estate was situated; the other two were Exeter, and Whitby on the Yorkshire coast.

It was the better part of an hour when the Count returned. "Aha!" he said. "Still at your books? Good! But you must not work always. Come, I am informed that your supper is ready." He took my arm, and we went into the next room, where I found an excellent supper ready on the table. The Count again excused himself, as he had dined out on his being away from home. But he sat as on the previous night, and chatted whilst I ate.

After supper I smoked, and the Count stayed with me, chatting and asking questions on every conceivable subject, hour after hour. I felt that it was getting very late indeed, but I did not say anything, for I felt under obligation to meet my host's wishes in every way. I was not sleepy, as the long sleep yesterday had fortified me, but I could not help experiencing that chill which comes over one at the coming of the dawn.

All at once we heard the crow of the cock coming up with preternatural shrillness through the clear morning air; Count Dracula, jumping to his feet, said, "Why, there is the morning again! How remiss I am to let you stay up so long." And with a courtly bow, he left me.

I went into my own room and drew the curtains, but there was little to notice; my window opened into the courtyard, all I could see was the warm grey of quickening sky. So I pulled the curtains again, and have written of this day.

8 *May* – I began to fear as I wrote in this book that I was getting too diffuse; but now I am glad that I went into detail from the first, for there is something so strange about this place that I cannot but feel uneasy. I wish I were safe out of it, or that I had never come. If there were anyone to talk to I could bear it, but there is no one. I have only the Count to speak with, and he! – I fear I am myself the only living soul within the place. Let me be prosaic so far as facts can be; it will help me to bear up, and imagination must not run riot with me. If it does I am lost. Let me say at once how I stand – or seem to.

I only slept a few hours when I went to bed, and feeling that I could not sleep any more, got up. I had hung my shaving glass by the window, and was just beginning to shave.

Suddenly I felt a hand on my shoulder, and heard the Count's voice saying to me, "Good morning."

I started, for it amazed me that I had not seen him, since the reflection of the glass covered the whole room behind me. In starting I had cut myself slightly, but did not notice it at the moment. Having answered the Count's salutation, I turned to the glass again to see how I had been mistaken. This time there could be no error, for the man was close to me, and I could see him over my shoulder.

But there was no reflection of him in the mirror! The whole room behind me was displayed; but there was no sign of a man in it, except myself.

At that instant I saw that the cut had bled a little, and the blood was trickling over my chin. I laid down the razor, turning as I did so half round to look for some sticking plaster.

When the Count saw my face, his eyes blazed with a sort of demoniac fury, and he suddenly made a grab at my throat. I drew away, and his hand touched the string of beads which held the crucifix. It made an instant change in him, for the fury passed so quickly that I could hardly believe that it was ever there.

"Take care," he said, "take care how you cut yourself. It is more dangerous than you think in this country."

Then seizing the shaving glass, he went on, "And this is the wretched thing that has done the mischief. It is a foul bauble of man's vanity. Away with it!" And opening the heavy window with one wrench of his terrible hand, he flung out the glass, which was shattered into a thousand pieces on the stones of the courtyard far below. Then he withdrew.

When I went into the dining-room, breakfast was prepared; but I could not find the Count anywhere, so I breakfasted alone. After breakfast I did a little exploring in the castle. I went out on the stairs and found a room looking towards the south.

The view was magnificent, and from where I stood there was every opportunity of seeing it. The castle is on the very edge of a terrible precipice. A stone falling from the window would fall a thousand feet without touching anything! As far as the eye can reach is a sea of green tree-tops, with occasionally a deep rift where there is a chasm. Here and there are silver threads where the rivers wind in deep gorges through the forests.

But I am not in heart to describe beauty, for when I had seen the view I explored further; doors, doors, doors everywhere, and all locked and bolted. In no place save from the windows in the castle walls is there an available exit.

The castle is a veritable prison, and I am a prisoner!

# 4

# Secrets of the Heart

*The very day after Jonathan Harker realized his terrifying predicament, his fiancée, Mina Murray, received her first letter from him. Posted before he had begun the last leg of his journey, the coach ride from Bistritz to the fearsome castle, it was brief, containing only hopeful news.*

*Mina, young, pale, fragile, overworked, could hardly wait for him to come home. But she had their wedding to look forward to, and before that, a holiday by the sea with her childhood friend Lucy Westenra. Mina was an assistant teacher, a tired one, and the sea air and long walks, she knew, would do her good.*

*Strangely, the girls were going to one of the places Count Dracula had ringed on his English map – Whitby, on the Yorkshire coast. Although she did not know it, Mina would see him there. Not as a man, however...*

*She wrote a letter to Lucy, who lived at Hillingham, near London. It was dated 9 May.*

My dearest Lucy,

Forgive my long delay in writing, but I have been simply overwhelmed with work. The life of an assistant schoolmistress is sometimes trying. I am longing to be with you, and by the sea, where we can talk together freely and build our castles in the air.

I have been working very hard lately, because I want to keep up with Jonathan's studies, and I have been practising shorthand very assiduously. When we are married I shall be able to be useful to Jonathan, and if I can stenograph well enough I can take down what he wants to say in this way and write it out for him on the typewriter, at which also I am practising very hard.

However, we shall see. I shall tell you all my little plans when we meet. I have just had a few hurried lines from Jonathan from Transylvania. He is well, and will be returning in about a week. I am longing to hear all his news. It must be so nice to see strange countries. I wonder if we – I mean Jonathan and I – shall ever see them together. There is the ten o'clock bell ringing. Goodbye.

Your loving

MINA

Tell me all the news when you write. You have not told me anything for a long time. I hear rumours, and especially of a tall, handsome, curly-haired man???

*Lucy's reply was very prompt – and full of vibrant life.*

17 *Chatham Street, Wednesday*

My dearest Mina,

I must say you tax me *very* unfairly with being a bad correspondent. I wrote to you *twice* since we parted, and your last letter was only your *second*. Besides, I have nothing to tell you. There is really nothing to interest you.

Town is very pleasant just now, and we go a good deal to picture-galleries and for walks and rides in the park. As to the tall, curly-haired man, someone has evidently been telling tales. That was Mr Holmwood. He often comes to see us, and he and Mamma get on very well together; they have so many things to talk about in common.

We met some time ago a man that would just *do for you*, if you were not already engaged to Jonathan. He is an excellent *parti*, being handsome, well off, and of good birth. He is a doctor and really clever. Just fancy! He is only nine-and-twenty, and he has an immense lunatic asylum all under his own care. Mr Holmwood introduced him to me, and he called here to see us, and often comes now. I think he is one of the most resolute men I ever saw, and yet the most calm.

I do not, as you know, take sufficient interest in dress to be able to describe the new fashions. Dress is a bore.

That is slang, but never mind; Arthur says that every day.

There, it is all out. Mina, we have told all our secrets to each other since we were *children*; we have slept together and eaten together, and laughed and cried together; and now, though I have spoken, I would like to speak more. Oh, Mina, couldn't you guess? I love him. I am blushing as I write, for although I *think* he loves me, he has not told me so in words. But, oh, Mina, I love him; I love him; I love him! There, that does me good.

I wish I were with you, dear, sitting by the fire undressing, as we used to sit; and I would try to tell you what I feel. I do not know how I am writing this even to you. I am afraid to stop, or I should tear up the letter, and I don't want to stop, for I *do so* want to tell you all.

Let me hear from you *at once*, and tell me all that you think about it. Mina, I must stop. Goodnight. Bless me in your prayers; and, Mina, pray for my happiness.

LUCY

P.S. I need not tell you this is a secret. Goodnight again. "L."

# 5

# The Lizard

After the mysterious and frightening incident with the shaving mirror, Jonathan Harker retreated into himself for some while. He had no explanation for the apparent phenomenon, but his thoughts were more exercised by the reality of his imprisonment, perhaps, than yet another strange event in a strange and awful land. He determined that he should talk to Dracula, to try to understand him, and they did indeed converse at length about the history of the area, and the Count's long and noble lineage.

Whatever his exact thoughts and feelings, however, he did not feel up to writing in his diary. When he did, some four days later, he stuck determinedly to mundane, concrete business matters – determinedly, and almost desperately.

It was not long, though, before more horrors came to shatter his morale. The next journal entry moves rapidly towards hysteria...

\*　　\*　　\*

## Jonathan Harker's Journal

12 May - Let me begin with facts - bare, meagre facts, verified by books and figures, and of which there can be no doubt. I must not confuse them with experiences which will have to rest on my own observation or my memory of them. Last evening when the Count came from his room he began by asking me questions on legal matters and on the doing of certain kinds of business.

First, he asked if a man in England might have two solicitors, or more. I told him he might have a dozen if he wished, but that it would not be wise to have more than one solicitor engaged in one transaction, as only one could act at a time, and that to change would be certain to militate against his interest.

He seemed thoroughly to understand, and went on to ask if there would be any practical difficulty in having one man to attend, say, to banking, and another to look after shipping, in case local help were needed in a place far from the home of the banking solicitor.

"Of course," I replied; "and such is often done by men of business who do not like the whole of their affairs to be known by any one person."

"Good!" he said, and then went on to ask about the means of making consignments and the forms to be gone through, and of all sorts of difficulties which might arise, but by forethought could be guarded against. When he had satisfied himself on these points, and I had verified all as well as I could by the books available, he suddenly stood up and said, "Have you written since your first letter to our friend Mr Peter Hawkins, or to any other?"

It was with some bitterness in my heart that I answered that I had not, that as yet I had not seen any opportunity of sending letters to anybody.

"Then write now, my young friend," he said, laying a heavy hand on my shoulder; "write to our friend and to any other; and say, if it will please you, that you shall stay with me until a month from now."

"Do you wish me to stay so long?" I asked, for my heart grew cold at the thought.

"I desire it much; nay, I will take no refusal. When your master, employer, what you will, engaged that someone should come on his behalf, it was understood that my needs only were to be consulted. I have not stinted. Is it not so?"

What could I do but bow acceptance? It was Mr Hawkins's interest, not mine, and I had to think of him, not myself; and besides, while Count Dracula was speaking, there was that in his eyes and in his bearing which made me remember that I was a prisoner, and could have no choice.

The Count saw his victory in my bow, and his mastery in the trouble of my face, for he began at once to use them, but in his own smooth, resistless way.

"I pray you, my good young friend, that you will not

discourse of things other than business in your letters. It will doubtless please your friends to know that you are well, and that you look forward to getting home to them. Is it not so?"

As he spoke he handed me three sheets of notepaper and three envelopes. They were all of the thinnest foreign post, and looking at them, then at him, and noticing his quiet smile, with the sharp, canine teeth lying over the red under-lip, I understood as well as if he had spoken that I should be careful what I wrote, for he would be able to read it. So I determined to write only formal notes now, but to write fully to Mr Hawkins in secret, and also to Mina, for to her I could write shorthand, which would puzzle the Count, if he did see it.

When I had written my two letters I sat quiet, reading a book whilst the Count wrote several notes, referring as he wrote them to some books on his table. Then he took up my two and placed them with his own, and turning to me, said, "I trust you will forgive me, but I have much work to do in private this evening. You will, I hope, find all things as you wish."

At the door he turned, and after a moment's pause said, "Let me advise you, my dear young friend - nay, let me warn you with all seriousness, that should you leave these rooms you will not by any chance go to sleep in any other part of the castle. It is old, and has many memories, and there are bad dreams for those who sleep unwisely. Be warned!"

"Should sleep now or ever overcome you, or be like to do, then haste to your own chamber or to these rooms, for your rest will then be safe. But if you be not careful in this respect, then—"

He finished his speech in a gruesome way, for he motioned with his hands as if he were washing them. I quite understood; my only doubt was as to whether any dream could be more terrible than the unnatural, horrible net of gloom and mystery which seemed closing round me.

*Later* – When he left me I went to my room. After a little while, not hearing any sound, I came out and went up the stone stair to where I could look out towards the south. There was some sense of freedom in the vast expanse, inaccessible though it was to me, as compared with the narrow darkness of the courtyard.

As I leaned from the window my eye was caught by something moving a storey below me, and somewhat to my left, where I imagined, from the lie of the rooms, that the windows of the Count's own room would look out. I drew back behind the stonework, and looked carefully out.

What I saw was the Count's head coming out from the window. I did not see the face, but I knew the man by the neck and the movement of his back and arms. I was at first interested, but my very feelings changed to repulsion and terror when I saw the whole man slowly emerge from the window and begin to crawl down the castle wall over that dreadful abyss, *face down*, with his cloak spreading out around him like great wings.

At first I could not believe my eyes. I thought it was some

trick of the moonlight, some weird effect of shadow; but I kept looking, and it could be no delusion. I saw the fingers and toes grasp the corners of the stones, worn clear of the mortar by the stress of years, and by thus using every projection and inequality move downwards with considerable speed, just as a lizard moves along a wall.

What manner of man is this, or what manner of creature is it in the semblance of man? I feel the dread of this horrible place overpowering me; I am in fear – in awful fear – and there is no escape for me.

I am encompassed about with terrors that I dare not think of...

# 6

# The First Seduction

*For three clear days after this awful shock, Jonathan again lay low. Confined to his room, consumed by fear, he sat down "as quietly as I have ever done anything in my life" and tried to work out what was happening, what everything might mean. He was fed and attended to solely by the Count, and had already concluded that there was no one else in the castle to do any task, however menial.*

*If there was no one else, he further realized, it must have been the Count himself who had been the driver of the coach that had brought him to the castle – and whom he had seen controlling savage wolves simply by holding up his hand. Which explained why the Bistritz people had been so afraid for him, and had tried to make him miss his rendezvous.*

*But on the evening of the third day, when he had once more watched Count Dracula clamber down the wall, obscenely upside down, Jonathan responded not with further terror, but with almighty courage. Dracula had quit the castle for a while, he reasoned. And despite the dreadful warnings – he would explore!*

*Taking a lamp, Jonathan set about trying doors, including the great door in the hall through which he had first entered Castle Dracula. All were locked, as he had expected, but he finally managed to force open one at the top of a stairway, which led him into a wing that, although dusty, seemed more comfortable than the rooms he was imprisoned in.*

*In fact, a "soft quietude" came over him, and he sat down at an oaken writing table, where he imagined "some fair lady" had sat in bygone times to write love letters, and began to catch up with his shorthand diary.*

*His next entry, written the morning afterwards, creeps with horror at the consequences of his actions. The horror built up very slowly.*

### Jonathan Harker's Journal

Later: the morning of 16 May – God preserve my sanity, for to this I am reduced. Safety and the assurance of safety are things of the past. Whilst I live on here there is but one thing to hope for: that I may not go mad, if, indeed, I be not mad already.

When I had written in my diary and had fortunately replaced the book and pen in my pocket, I felt sleepy. The Count's warning came into my mind, but I took a pleasure in disobeying it. I determined not to return tonight to the gloom-haunted rooms, but to sleep here, where, of old, ladies had sat and sung and lived sweet lives whilst their gentle breasts were sad for their menfolk away in the midst of remorseless wars.

I drew a great couch out of its place near the corner, so that, as I lay, I could look at the lovely view to east and south, and unthinking of and uncaring for the dust, composed myself for sleep.

I suppose I must have fallen asleep; I hope so, but I fear; for all that followed was startlingly real – so real that now, sitting here in the broad, full sunlight of the morning, I cannot in the least believe that it was all sleep.

I was not alone. In the moonlight opposite me were three young women, ladies by their dress and manner. I thought at the time that I must be dreaming when I saw them, for, though the moonlight was behind them, they threw no shadow on the floor. They came close to me and looked at me for some time, and then whispered together.

Two were dark, and had high aquiline noses, like the Count, and great dark, piercing eyes, that seemed to be almost red when contrasted with the pale yellow moon. The other was fair, as fair as can be, with great, wavy masses of golden hair and eyes like pale sapphires. I seemed somehow to know her face, and to know it in connection with some dreamy fear, but I could not recollect at the moment how or where.

All three had brilliant white teeth, that shone like pearls against the ruby of their voluptuous lips. There was something about them that made me uneasy, some longing and at the same time some deadly fear. I felt in my heart a wicked, burning desire that they would kiss me with those red lips. It is not good to note this down, lest some day it should meet Mina's eyes and cause her pain; but it is the truth.

They whispered together, and then they all three laughed – such a silvery, musical laugh, but as hard as though the sound never could have come through the softness of human lips. The fair girl shook her head coquettishly, and the other two urged her on.

One said, "Go on! You are first, and we shall follow; yours is the right to begin."

The other added, "He is young and strong; there are kisses for us all."

I lay quiet, looking out under my eyelashes in an agony of delightful anticipation. The fair girl advanced and bent over me till I could feel the movement of her breath upon me. Sweet it was in one sense, honey-sweet, and sent the same tingling through the nerves as her voice, but with a bitter underlying the sweet, a bitter offensiveness, as one smells in blood.

I was afraid to raise my eyelids, but looked out and saw perfectly under the lashes. The fair girl went on her knees, and bent over me, fairly gloating. There was a deliberate voluptuousness which was both thrilling and repulsive, and as she arched her neck she actually licked her lips like an animal, till I could see in the moonlight the moisture shining on the scarlet lips and on the red tongue as it lapped the white sharp teeth.

Lower and lower went her head as the lips went below the range of my mouth and chin and seemed about to fasten on my throat. Then she paused, and I could feel the hot breath on my neck, the soft, shivering touch of the lips on the supersensitive skin of my throat, the hard dents of two sharp teeth, just touching and pausing there. I closed my eyes in a languorous ecstasy and waited – waited with beating heart.

But at that instant another sensation swept through me as quick as lightning. I was conscious of the presence of the Count, and of his being in a storm of fury. As my eyes opened involuntarily I saw his strong hand grasp the slender neck of the fair woman and with giant's power draw it back, the blue eyes transformed with fury.

But the Count! Never did I imagine such wrath and fury, even in the demons of the pit. His eyes were positively blazing. The red light in them was lurid, as if the flames of hellfire blazed behind them.

With a fierce sweep of his arm, he hurled the woman from him, and then motioned to the others, as though he were beating them back; it was the same imperious gesture that I had seen used to the wolves.

In a voice which, though low and almost in a whisper, seemed to cut through the air and then ring round the room, he said, "How dare you touch him, any of you? How dare you cast eyes on him when I had forbidden it? Back, I tell you all! This man belongs to me! Beware how you meddle with him, or you'll have to deal with me."

The fair girl, with a laugh of ribald coquetry, turned to answer him.

"You yourself never loved; you never love!" On this the other women joined, and such a mirthless, hard, soulless laughter rang through the room that it almost made me faint to hear; it seemed like the pleasure of fiends.

Then the Count turned, after looking at my face attentively, and said in a soft whisper, "Yes, I too can love; you yourselves can tell it from the past. Is it not so? Well, now I promise you that when I am done with him you shall kiss him at your will. Now go! Go! I must awaken him, for there is work to be done."

"Are we to have nothing tonight?" said one of them, as she pointed to the bag which he had thrown upon the floor, and which moved as though there were some living thing within it.

For answer he nodded his head. One of the women jumped forward and opened it. If my ears did not deceive me there was a gasp and a low wail, as of a half-smothered child. The women closed round, whilst I was aghast with horror. But as I looked they disappeared; and with them the dreadful bag.

There was no door near them, and they could not have passed me without my noticing. They simply seemed to fade into the rays of the moonlight and pass out through the window, for I could see outside the dim, shadowy forms for a moment before they entirely faded away.

Then the horror overcame me, and I sank down unconscious.

# 7

# A Date with Execution

## Jonathan Harker's Journal

16 May - I awoke in my own bed. If it be that I had not dreamt, the Count must have carried me here. I tried to satisfy myself on the subject, but could not arrive at any unquestionable result.

To be sure, there were certain small evidences, such as that my clothes were folded and laid by in a manner which was not my habit. My watch was still unwound, and I am rigorously accustomed to wind it the last thing before going to bed, and many such details.

But these things are no proof, for they may have been evidences that my mind was not as usual, and, for some cause or another, I had certainly been much upset. I must watch for proof.

Of one thing I am glad: if it was that the Count carried me here and undressed me, he must have been hurried in his task, for my pockets are intact. I am sure this diary would have been a mystery to him which he would not have brooked. He would have taken or destroyed it.

As I look round this room, although it has been to me so full of fear, it is now a sort of sanctuary, for nothing can be more dreadful than those awful women, who were – who *are* – waiting to suck my blood.

*18 May* – I have been down to look at that room again in day-light, for I *must* know the truth. When I got to the doorway at the top of the stairs I found it closed. It had been so forcibly driven against the jamb that part of the woodwork was splin-tered. I could see that the bolt of the lock had not been shot, but the door is fastened from the inside. I fear it was no dream, and must act on this surmise.

*19 May* – I am surely in the toils. Last night the Count asked me in the suavest tones to write three letters, one saying that my work here was nearly done, and that I should start for home within a few days, another that I was starting on the next morning from the time of the letter, and the third that I had left the castle and arrived at Bistritz.

He explained to me that posts were few and uncertain, and that my writing now would ensure ease of mind to my friends. I pretended to fall in with his views, and asked him what dates I should put on the letters.

He calculated a minute, and then said, "The first should be 12 June, the second 19 June, and the third 29 June."

I know now the span of my life. God help me!

# 8

# The Intertwining Fates

Jonathan's letters, he understood, would be sent from Transylvania by Dracula on the chosen dates to hide the truth of his real whereabouts and to wreak confusion at home long after he was safely dead. In those times, despite the Count's excuses, the postal service was in fact efficient and reliable, with many deliveries a day in London and elsewhere, ideal for spreading information, true or false. Indeed, unbeknown to Jonathan, other news that would turn out to be of great importance in all their lives was already criss-crossing England.

A few days after he penned his false notes for the Count, Mina – who craved letters from no one but her poor fiancé – received one not from him, but from Lucy Westenra. The flirtatious, jolly, rich girl had at last made up her mind about her future – and had, of course, to share it with her best friend.

The letter was dated 24 May.

My dearest Mina,

Thanks, and thanks, and thanks again for your sweet letter! It was so nice to be able to tell you and to have your sympathy.

My dear, it never rains but it pours. How true the old proverbs are. Here am I, who shall be twenty in September, and yet I never had a proposal till today, not a real proposal, and today I have had three.

Just fancy! THREE proposals in one day! Isn't it awful! I feel sorry, really and truly sorry, for two of the poor fellows. Oh, Mina, I am so happy that I don't know what to do with myself. And three proposals!

*John Seward, the asylum owner, had been the first one to ask if she would marry him, and it had moved Lucy to tears ("excuse this letter being all blotted") to have to turn him down. He was outwardly very cool, she told Mina, and unfailingly polite, although he did keep playing with a razor-sharp surgeon's scalpel "in a way that made me nearly scream."*

*He was very brave when she rejected him, however, and after lunch she felt strong enough to meet Number Two, a rich young Texan called Quincey P. Morris.*

*Although a very jolly sort of man, Morris was not short of passion, and suddenly began "pouring out a perfect torrent of love-making", laying his heart and soul at Lucy's feet. And then he stopped, seeing something in her eyes, perhaps, and asked her if there was already someone that she "cared for". Lucy burst into tears, but she did manage to admit that it was true.*

*Then – and this was Queen Victoria's strait-laced reign, remember – she kissed him. Mr Quincey Morris "wrung my hand, and taking up his hat, went straight out of the room without looking back" – a perfect English gentleman, and a Texan too! Lucy, however, seemed to have got the taste for kissing, as her postscript reveals without a maiden blush:*

P.S. Oh, about number three – I needn't tell you of number three, need I? Besides, it was all so confused; it seemed only a moment from his coming into the room till both his arms were round me, and he was kissing me. I am very, very happy, and I don't know what I have done to deserve it. I must only try in the future to show that I am not ungrateful to God for all His goodness to me in sending to me such a lover, such a husband, and such a friend.

Goodbye.

*Number Three, of course, was the Honourable Arthur Holmwood, a friend and co-adventurer to both Quincey and Jack Seward. For many years the three of them had done everything together, had shared many world adventures. Now their destinies and Lucy's were to be, it seemed, forever intertwined.*

*Strangely – and one can only speculate that Dracula,*

somehow, was directing these events in a supernatural way –
Jack Seward was the owner of the lunatic asylum next door to
Carfax, which was the property the Count had just bought
through Jonathan Harker and his firm. Dracula had a helper
there, an inmate who was waiting for him to come back. For
Seward, soon the strands would start to mesh, most horribly.

In the meantime, though, after his disappointment over
Lucy, the doctor could not eat and could not rest, and so
immersed himself in work. He told his diary – recorded onto
phonographic cylinders, the nineteenth-century precursor to the
tape recorder – that he chose to study the interesting inmate,
R. M. Renfield, aged 59, to take his mind off things.

*Renfield, he said, was "of sanguine temperament; great physical strength; morbidly excitable; periods of gloom ending in some fixed idea which I cannot make out." He was also "quaint in his ideas", and "unlike the normal lunatic".*

*He was, though, possibly – or even probably – "a dangerous man".*

*Just how dangerous would be emerging very soon.*

# 9

# The Living Corpse

Jonathan's despair, after he learned that he was to die on 29 June or thereabouts, was overwhelming. His journal remained untouched for nine clear days, and the next entry revealed only more disasters.

A band of Szgany, a gypsy-like tribe, had come into the castle courtyard, no doubt called there by the Count, and Jonathan had tried to bribe them to take away and post two letters that he had written in secret – one to Mina Murray and the other to his employer, Mr Hawkins.

He threw the letters, and a piece of gold, down to one of the Szgany, who "pressed them to his heart and bowed". Shortly afterwards, Dracula walked into Jonathan's room, all smiles, and opened the same two letters as he watched.

The one to Hawkins, simply asking that he get in touch with Mina, Dracula insisted that Jonathan should put in a new envelope – it would be sent, he said.

Mina's was in shorthand, though – "a vile thing, an outrage

*upon friendship and hospitality!" – and he burned it to ashes as Jonathan looked on.*

*Three days later, Jonathan recorded, he found that the Count had taken every scrap of paper from his bag, as well as all his envelopes, travel documents and letters of credit.*

*From his wardrobe, he then discovered, he had lost his travelling suit and his overcoat. He realized that Dracula must have taken his clothes to leave the castle in, so that there would be eyewitnesses to say the Englishman had been seen outside the walls, free to come and go.*

*Vile acts were also committed in this disguise for the same reason – to incriminate him as the perpetrator. One awful night he heard a little child wailing somewhere in the castle, then the agonized cry of a woman in the courtyard.*

*He noted in his journal:* I rushed to the window, and throwing it up, peered out between the bars. There, indeed, was a woman with dishevelled hair, holding her hands over her heart as one distressed with running. She was leaning against a corner of the gateway. When she saw my face at the window she threw herself forward, and shouted in a voice laden with menace, "Monster, give me my child!"

She threw herself on her knees, and raising up her hands, cried the same words in tones which wrung my heart. Then she tore her hair and beat her breast, and abandoned herself to all the violences of extravagant emotion. Finally, she threw herself forward, and, though I could not see her, I could hear the beating of her naked hands against the door.

Somewhere high overhead, probably on the tower, I heard the voice of the Count calling in his harsh, metallic whisper. His call seemed to be answered from far and wide by the howling of wolves. Before many minutes had passed a pack of them poured, like a pent-up dam when liberated, through the wide entrance into the courtyard.

There was no cry from the woman, and the howling of the wolves was but short. Before long they streamed away singly, licking their lips.

I could not pity her, for I knew now what had become of her child, and she was better dead.

What shall I do? What can I do? How can I escape from this dreadful thrall of night and gloom and fear?

Earlier that day, and for several days before, Jonathan had heard the muffled sound of digging, which he guessed was being done for Dracula by the Szgany band. On 17 June he had seen them take delivery of a quantity of "great, square boxes, with handles of thick rope" that arrived on two "leiter-wagons", each drawn by eight horses and led by high-booted Slovaks.

The boxes – empty, judging by the ease with which the Slovaks handled them – were presumably being filled with something deep down in the cellars of the castle.

It was the death of the child and mother, though, that spurred Jonathan Harker, finally, to action. When the sun *arose the next morning, it filled him with new hope, and great determination.*

## Jonathan Harker's Journal

*25 June, morning* – No man knows till he has suffered from the night how sweet and dear to his heart and eye the morning can be. When the sun grew so high this morning that it struck the top of the great gateway opposite my window, my fear fell from me as if it had been a vaporous garment which dissolved in the warmth.

I must take action of some sort whilst the courage of the day is upon me. Last night one of my post-dated letters went to post, the first of that fatal series which is to blot out the very traces of my existence from the earth.

Let me not think of it. Action!

It has always been at night-time that I have been molested or threatened, or in some way in danger or in fear. I have not yet seen the Count in the daylight. Can it be that he sleeps when others wake, that he may be awake whilst they sleep? If I could only get into his room! But there is no possible way. The door is always locked, no way for me.

Yes, there is a way, if one dares to take it. Where his body has gone why may not another body go? I have seen him myself crawl from his window; why should not I imitate him, and go in by his window? The chances are desperate, but my need is more desperate still.

*Same day, later* – I have made the effort, and, God helping me, have come safely back to this room. I must put down every detail in order.

I went whilst my courage was fresh straight to the window on the south side, and at once got outside on the narrow ledge. The stones were big and roughly cut, and the mortar had by process of time been washed away between them.

I took off my boots, and ventured out on the desperate way. I looked down once, so as to make sure that a sudden glimpse of the awful depth would not overcome me, but after that kept my eyes away from it.

I knew pretty well the direction and distance of the Count's window, and made for it as well as I could, having regard to the opportunities available. I did not feel dizzy – I suppose I was too excited – and the time seemed ridiculously short till I found myself standing on the windowsill and trying to raise up the sash. I was filled with agitation, however, when I bent down and slid feet foremost in through the window. Then I looked around for the Count, but, with surprise and gladness, made a discovery.

The room was empty! The only thing I found was a great heap of gold in one corner – gold of all kinds, Roman, and British, and Austrian, and Hungarian, and Greek and Turkish money, covered with a film of dust. There were also chains and ornaments, some jewelled, but all of them old and stained.

At one corner of the room was a heavy door. I tried it,

for, since I could not find the key of the room or the key of the outer door, I must make further examination, or all my efforts would be in vain. It was open, and led through a stone passage to a circular stairway, which went steeply down.

I descended, minding carefully where I went, for the stairs were dark, being only lit by loopholes in the heavy masonry. At the bottom there was a dark, tunnel-like passage, through which came a deathly, sickly odour, the odour of old earth newly turned. As I went through the passage the smell grew closer and heavier.

At last I pulled open a heavy door which stood ajar, and found myself in an old, ruined chapel, which had evidently been used as a graveyard. The roof was broken, and in two places were steps leading to vaults, but the ground had recently been dug over, and the earth placed in great wooden boxes, manifestly those which had been brought by the Slovaks.

I went down even into the vaults, where the dim light struggled, although to do so was a dread to my very soul. Into two of these I went, but saw nothing except fragments of old coffins and piles of dust; in the third, however, I made a discovery.

There, in one of the great boxes, of which there were fifty in all, on a pile of newly dug earth, lay the Count!

He was either dead or asleep, I could not say which - for the eyes were open and stony, but without the glassiness of

death – and the cheeks had the warmth of life through all their pallor, and the lips were as red as ever. But there was no sign of movement, no pulse, no breath, no beating of the heart.

I bent over him, and tried to find any sign of life, but in

vain. He could not have lain there long, for the earthy smell would have passed away in a few hours. By the side of the box was its cover, pierced with holes here and there.

I thought he might have the keys on him, but when I went to search I saw the dead eyes, and in them, dead though they were, such a look of hate, though unconscious of me or my presence, that I fled from the place, and leaving the Count's room by the window, crawled again up the castle wall. Regaining my own chamber, I threw myself panting upon the bed and tried to think...

# 10

# Over the Precipice

*The next four days are silence in the shorthand journal. Jonathan Harker, alone and crushed, overwhelmed by the horror of his discovery, can, it seems, do nothing more. He sleeps, and when awake he reads until he sleeps once more.*

*The next entry comes on 29 June – a date, in his short life, of appalling significance. There is only one more entry after it. Then, for Jonathan, there is nothing ... except the precipice.*

## Jonathan Harker's Journal

*29 June* – Today is the date of my last letter, and the Count has taken steps to prove that it was genuine, for again I saw him leave the castle by the same window, and in my clothes.

As he went down the wall, lizard fashion, I wished I had a gun or some lethal weapon, that I might destroy him; but I fear that no weapon wrought alone by man's hand would have any effect on him.

I dared not wait to see him return, for I feared to see those weird sisters. I came back to the library, and read there till I fell asleep.

I was awakened by the Count, who looked at me as grimly as a man can look as he said, "Tomorrow, my friend, we must part. You return to your beautiful England, I to some work which may have such an end that we may never meet. Your letter home has been despatched: tomorrow I shall not be here, but all shall be ready for your journey.

"In the morning come the Szgany, who have some labours of their own here, and also come some Slovaks. When they have gone, my carriage shall come for you, and shall bear you to the Borgo Pass to meet the diligence from Bukovina to Bistritz. But I am in hopes that I shall see more of you at Castle Dracula."

I suspected him, and determined to test his sincerity. Sincerity! It seems like a profanation of the word to write it in connection with such a monster, so I asked him point-blank: "Why may I not go tonight?"

"Because, dear sir, my coachman and horses are away on a mission."

"But I would walk with pleasure. I want to get away at once."

He smiled, such a soft, smooth, diabolical smile that I knew there was some trick behind his smoothness. He said, "And your baggage?"

"I do not care about it. I can send for it some other time."

The Count stood up, and said, with a sweet courtesy which made me rub my eyes, it seemed so real, "Come with me, my dear young friend. Not an hour shall you wait in my house against your will, though sad am I at your going, and that you so suddenly desire it. Come!"

With a stately gravity, he, with the lamp, preceded me down the stairs and along the hall. Suddenly he stopped.

"Hark!"

Close at hand came the howling of many wolves. It was almost as if the sound sprang up at the raising of his hand, just as the music of a great orchestra seems to leap under the bâton of the conductor. After a pause of a moment, he proceeded, in his stately way, to the door, drew back the ponderous bolts, unhooked the heavy chains, and began to draw it open.

As the door began to open, the howling of the wolves without grew louder and angrier; their red jaws, with champing teeth, and their blunt-clawed feet as they leaped, came in through the opening door.

Suddenly it struck me that this might be the moment and the means of my doom; I was to be given to the wolves, and at my own instigation. There was a diabolical wickedness in the idea great enough for the Count, and as a last chance I cried out, "Shut the door; I shall wait till morning!" and covered my face with my hands to hide my tears of bitter disappointment.

With one sweep of his powerful arm, the Count threw the door shut, and the great bolts clanged and echoed through the hall as they shot back into their places.

In silence we returned to the library, and after a minute or two I went to my own room. The last I saw of Count Dracula was his kissing his hand to me, with a red light of triumph in his eyes and with a smile that Judas in hell might be proud of.

When I was in my room and about to lie down, I thought I heard a whispering at my door. I went to it softly and listened. Unless my ears deceived me, I heard the voice of the Count, "Back, back, to your own place! Your time is not yet come. Wait! Have patience. Tomorrow night, tomorrow night, is yours!"

There was a low, sweet ripple of laughter, and in a rage I threw open the door, and saw without the three terrible women licking their lips. As I appeared they all joined in a horrible laugh, and ran away.

I came back to my room and threw myself on my knees. Is it then so near the end? Tomorrow! Tomorrow! Lord, help me, and those to whom I am dear!

*30 June, morning* – These may be the last words I ever write in this diary. I slept till just before the dawn, and when I woke threw myself on my knees, for I determined that if Death came he should find me ready.

At last I felt that subtle change in the air, and I knew that the morning had come. Then came the welcome cock-crow, and I felt that I was safe. With a glad heart, I opened my door and ran down to the hall. I had seen that the door was unlocked, and now escape was before me. With hands that trembled with eagerness, I unhooked the chains and threw back the massive bolts.

But the door would not move. Despair seized me. I pulled and pulled, and shook it till it rattled. It had been locked after I left the Count.

Then a wild desire took me to obtain that key at any risk, and I determined then and there to scale the wall again and gain the Count's room. Without a pause I rushed up to the east window, and scrambled down the wall, as before, into the room.

It was empty, but that was as I expected. I could not see a key anywhere. I went through the door in the corner and down the winding stair and along the dark passage to the old chapel. I knew now well enough where to find the monster I sought.

The great box was in the same place, close against the wall, but the lid was laid on it, not fastened down, but with the nails ready in their places to be hammered home.

I knew I must search the body for the key, so I raised the lid, and laid it back against the wall; and then I saw something which filled my very soul with horror.

There lay the Count, but looking as if his youth had been

half renewed, for the white hair and moustache were changed to dark iron-grey; the cheeks were fuller, and the white skin seemed ruby-red underneath; the mouth was redder than ever, for on the lips were gouts of fresh blood, which trickled from the corners of the mouth and ran down over the chin and neck.

Even the deep, burning eyes seemed set amongst swollen flesh, for the lids and pouches underneath were bloated. It seemed as if the whole awful creature were simply gorged with blood; he lay like a filthy leech, exhausted with his repletion.

I shuddered as I bent over to touch him, and every sense in me revolted at the contact; but I had to search, or I was lost. The coming night might see my own body a banquet in a similar way to those horrid three.

I felt all over the body, but no sign could I find of the key. Then I stopped and looked at the Count. There was a mocking smile on the bloated face which seemed to drive me mad.

This was the being I was helping to transfer to London, where, perhaps, for centuries to come he might, amongst its teeming millions, satiate his lust for blood, and create a new and ever-widening circle of semi-demons to batten on the helpless.

The very thought drove me mad. A terrible desire came upon me to rid the world of such a monster. There was no lethal weapon at hand, but I seized a shovel which the workmen had been using to fill the cases, and lifting it high, struck, with the edge downward, at the hateful face.

But as I did so the head turned, and the eyes fell full upon me, with all their blaze of basilisk horror. The sight seemed to paralyse me, and the shovel turned in my hand and glanced from the face, merely making a deep gash above the forehead.

The shovel fell from my hand across the box, and as I pulled it away the flange of the blade caught the edge of the lid, which fell over again, and hid the horrid thing from my sight. The last glimpse I had was of the bloated face, blood-stained and fixed with a grin of malice which would have held its own in the nethermost hell.

I thought and thought what should be my next move, but my brain seemed on fire, and I waited with a despairing feeling growing over me. As I waited I heard in the distance a gypsy song sung by merry voices coming closer, and through their song the rolling of heavy wheels and the cracking of whips; the Szgany and the Slovaks of whom the Count had spoken were coming.

With a last look around and at the box which contained the vile body, I ran from the place and gained the Count's room.

Then there came the sound of many feet tramping and dying away in some passage which sent up a clanging echo. I turned to run down again towards the vault, but at the moment there seemed to come a violent puff of wind, and the door to the winding stair blew to with a shock that set the dust from the lintels flying.

When I ran to push it open, I found that it was hopelessly fast. I was again a prisoner, and the net of doom was closing round me more closely.

As I write there is in the passage below a sound of many tramping feet and the crash of weights being set down heavily, doubtless the boxes, with their freight of earth. There is a sound of hammering; it is the box being nailed down. Now I can hear the heavy feet tramping again along the hall, with many other idle feet coming behind them.

The door is shut, and the chains rattle; there is a grinding of the key in the lock; I can hear the key withdrawn; then another door opens and shuts; I hear the creaking of lock and bolt.

Hark! In the courtyard and down the rocky way the roll of heavy wheels, the crack of whips, and the chorus of the Szgany as they pass into the distance.

I am alone in the castle with those awful women. Faugh! Mina is a woman, and there is nought in common. They are devils of the Pit!

I shall not remain alone with them; I shall try to scale the castle wall farther than I have yet attempted. I shall take some of the gold with me, lest I want it later. I may find a way from this dreadful place.

And then away for home! Away to the quickest and nearest train! Away from this cursed spot, from this cursed land, where the devil and his children still walk with earthly feet!

At least God's mercy is better than that of these monsters,

and the precipice is steep and high. At its foot a man may sleep – as a man.

Goodbye, all! Mina!

Book Two
THE FALL of
LUCY WESTENRA

*1*

# Storm Clouds Gather

The ship that had been charted by Dracula to carry the fifty boxes full of earth – and one of them, also, his "Un-Dead" remains – left the Black Sea port of Varna bound for the Yorkshire coast of England early in July.

She was a sailing ship, a schooner called the Demeter, and she made an amazingly fast passage. Even more amazingly, the man who steered her into Whitby harbour was a corpse, tied to the wheel.

Before the ship arrived, however, Lucy Westenra and her friend Mina – still waiting forlornly for good news of her love – had already moved into their rented rooms to spend their *holiday. Lucy had come up first, with her mother, and she had met Mina off the Exeter train.*

*So far, in her journal, Mina had written only first impressions of the town.*

### Mina Murray's Journal

24 July, Whitby – Lucy met me at the station, looking sweeter and lovelier than ever, and we drove up to the house at the Crescent in which they have rooms.

This is a lovely place. The little river, the Esk, runs through a deep valley, which broadens out as it comes near the harbour. The houses of the old town – the side away from us – are all red-roofed, and seem piled up one over the other anyhow, like the pictures we see of Nuremberg.

Right over the town is the ruin of Whitby Abbey, which was sacked by the Danes. It is a most noble ruin, of immense size, and full of beautiful and romantic bits; between it and the town there is another church, the Parish one, round which is a big graveyard, all full of tombstones.

This is to my mind the nicest spot in Whitby, for it has a full view of the harbour and all up the bay to where the headland called Kettleness stretches out into the sea.

I shall come and sit here often and work. Indeed, I am writing now, with my book on my knee, and listening to the talk of three old men who are sitting beside me. They seem to do nothing all day but sit up here and talk.

Lucy went out visiting with her mother, and as they were only duty calls, I did not go.

*Within two days, though, an anxious note was creeping into Mina's shorthand writings. She had received a letter from Jonathan, finally – via Mr Hawkins, in Exeter – but somehow it did not sound right.*

*"It is only a line dated from Castle Dracula," she wrote, "and says that he is just starting for home. That is not like Jonathan; I do not understand it, and it makes me uneasy."*

*Although she does not mention a date, the letter was probably that of 19 June, the second one the Count had made him write. By this time, Mina was aware, her fiancé should have already been back home for days, if not weeks.*

*Lucy, also, was giving cause for worry.*

## *Mina Murray's Journal*

26 July – Then, too, Lucy, although she is so well, has lately taken to her old habit of walking in her sleep. Her mother has spoken to me about it, and we have decided that I am to lock the door of our room every night.

Mrs Westenra has got an idea that sleepwalkers always go out on roofs of houses and along the edges of cliffs, and then get suddenly wakened and fall over with a despairing cry that echoes all over the place. Poor dear, she is naturally anxious.

Lucy is to be married in the autumn, and she is already

planning out her dresses and how her house is to be arranged. I sympathise with her, for I do the same, only Jonathan and I will start in life in a very simple way, and shall have to try to make both ends meet.

Mr Holmwood - he is the Hon. Arthur Holmwood, only son of Lord Godalming - is coming up here very shortly - as soon as he can leave town, for his father is not very well, and I think dear Lucy is counting the moments till he comes.

She wants to take him up to the seat on the churchyard cliff and show him the beauty of Whitby. I daresay it is the waiting which disturbs her; she will be all right when he arrives.

*Holmwood, then, the successful competitor for Lucy's hand, turns out to be "the Honourable", and a lord's son. Both he and Quincey Morris, in fact, were extremely wealthy – men of leisure.*

*The third suitor, however – the asylum owner Dr Seward – had to work. And as the ship carrying Dracula on his bed of filthy earth got ever closer to England, the condition of his strangest patient became ever more bizarre.*

# 2

# The Man Who Ate Life

## Dr Seward's Diary

*5 June* – The case of Renfield grows more interesting the more I get to understand the man. He seems to have some settled scheme of his own, but what it is I do not yet know. His redeeming quality is a love of animals, though, indeed, he has such curious turns in it that I sometimes imagine he is only abnormally cruel. His pets are of odd sorts. Just now his hobby is catching flies. He has at present such a quantity that I have had myself to expostulate. To my astonishment, he did not break out into a fury, as I expected, but took the matter in simple seriousness. He thought for a moment, and then said, "May I have three days? I shall clear them away." Of course, I said that would do. I must watch him.

*18 June* – He has turned his mind now to spiders, and has got several very big fellows in a box. He keeps feeding them with his flies, and the number of the latter is becoming sensibly diminished, although he has used half his food in attracting more.

*1 July* – His spiders are now becoming as great a nuisance as his flies, and today I told him that he must get rid of them. He looked very sad at this, so I said that he must clear out some of them, at all events. He cheerfully acquiesced in this, and I gave him the same time as before for reduction.

He disgusted me much while with him, for when a horrid blow-fly, bloated with some carrion food, buzzed into the room, he caught it, held it exultingly for a few moments between his finger and thumb, and, before I knew what he was going to do, put it in his mouth and ate it.

I scolded him for it, but he argued quietly that it was very good and very wholesome; that it was life, strong life, and gave life to him. This gave me an idea, or the rudiment of one. I must watch how he gets rid of his spiders.

*8 July* – There is a method in his madness, and the rudimentary idea in my mind is growing. I kept away for a few days, so that I might notice if there were any change. He has managed to get a sparrow, and has already partially tamed it. His means of taming is simple, for already the spiders have

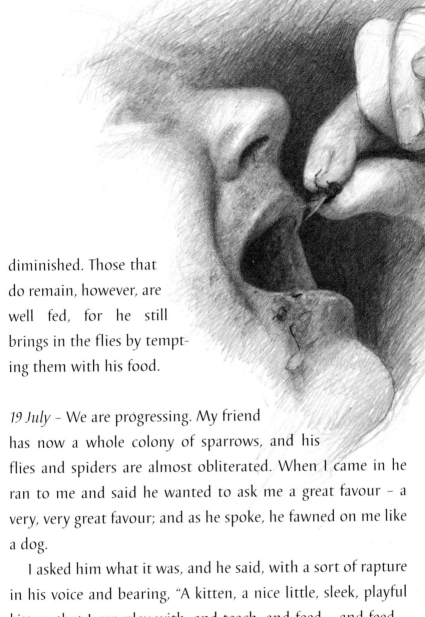

diminished. Those that
do remain, however, are
well fed, for he still
brings in the flies by tempt-
ing them with his food.

*19 July* – We are progressing. My friend
has now a whole colony of sparrows, and his
flies and spiders are almost obliterated. When I came in he
ran to me and said he wanted to ask me a great favour – a
very, very great favour; and as he spoke, he fawned on me like
a dog.

I asked him what it was, and he said, with a sort of rapture
in his voice and bearing, "A kitten, a nice little, sleek, playful
kitten, that I can play with, and teach, and feed – and feed –
and feed!"

I was not unprepared for this request, for I had noticed
how his pets went on increasing in size and vivacity, but I did

not care that his pretty family of tame sparrows should be wiped out in the same manner as the flies and spiders; so I said I would see about it, and asked him if he would not rather have a cat than a kitten.

His eagerness betrayed him. "Oh yes, I would like a cat! I only asked for a kitten lest you should refuse me a cat. No one would refuse me a kitten, would they?"

I shook my head, and said that at present I feared it would not be possible, but that I would see about it. His face fell, and I could see a warning of danger in it, for there was a sudden fierce, sidelong look which meant killing. The man is an undeveloped homicidal maniac. I shall test him with his present craving and see how it will work out; then I shall know more.

*20 July* – Visited Renfield very early, before the attendant went his rounds. Found him up and humming a tune. He was spreading out his sugar, which he had saved, in the window, and was manifestly beginning his fly-catching again; and beginning it cheerfully and with a good grace.

I looked around for his birds, and not seeing them, asked him where they were. He replied, without turning round, that they had all flown away. There were a few feathers about the room and on his pillow a drop of blood. I said nothing.

*11 a.m.* – The attendant has just been to see me to say that Renfield has been very sick and has disgorged a whole lot of feathers. "My belief is, doctor," he said, "that he has eaten his birds, and that he just took and ate them raw!"

*11 p.m.* – I gave Renfield a strong opiate tonight, enough to make even him sleep, and took away his pocket-book to look at it. The thought that has been buzzing about my brain lately is complete, and the theory proved.

My homicidal maniac is of a peculiar kind. I shall have to invent a new classification for him, and call him a zoophagous (life-eating) maniac; what he desires is to absorb as many lives as he can, and he has laid himself out to achieve it in a cumulative way. He gave many flies to one spider and many spiders to one bird, and then wanted a cat to eat the many birds. What would have been his later steps?

It would almost be worthwhile to complete the experiment. I wonder at how many lives he values a man, or if at only one. He has closed the account most accurately, and today begun a new record. How many of us begin a new record with each day of our lives?

# 3

# The Coffin Ship Arrives

Although she had no inkling that the schooner Demeter was rushing towards the coast of Yorkshire, Mina Murray recorded in her diary, from 27 July onward, a great and growing feeling of some impending doom.

There was still no news from Jonathan; she was being woken every single night by a restless Lucy "moving about the room"; and Mr Holmwood's father had taken a turn for the worse, which meant Arthur would not be coming to join his fiancée until later than they had all hoped.

One week further on, and the situation had deteriorated.

## *Mina Murray's Journal*

*3 August* – No news from Jonathan, not even to Mr Hawkins, from whom I have heard. Oh, I do hope he is not ill.

Lucy has not walked much in her sleep the last week, but there is an odd concentration about her which I do not understand; even in her sleep she seems to be watching me. She tries the door, and finding it locked, goes about the room searching for the key.

*6 August* – Another three days. This suspense is getting dreadful. If I only knew where to write to or where to go to, I should feel easier; but no one has heard a word of Jonathan since that last letter. I must only pray to God for patience.

Lucy is more excitable than ever, but is otherwise well. Last night was very threatening, and the fishermen say that we are in for a storm. I must try to watch it and learn the weather signs.

*Mina did observe the signs, by walking to the cemetery and staring out at the water, which was "tumbling in over the shallows with a roar, muffled in the sea-mists." She also spoke to Mr Swales, an ancient local man she had befriended – and he was far from his usual cheerful self.*

*There was something in the wind, he told her, and it "smells like death". He felt that he would very soon be gone...*

*Mina was moved to tears, and the pair were silent for a while. Then Mr Swales got up, shook hands with her and blessed her. He said goodbye, and "hobbled off".*

It all touched me *(Mina wrote)*, and upset me very much. I was glad when the coastguard came along, with his spyglass under his arm. He stopped to talk with me, as he always does, but all the time kept looking at a strange ship.

"I can't make her out," he said; "she's a Russian, by the look of her; but she's knocking about in the queerest way. She doesn't know her mind a bit; she seems to see the storm coming, but can't decide whether to run up north in the open, or to put in here.

"Look there again! She is steered mighty strangely, for she changes about with every puff of wind. We'll hear more of her before this time tomorrow."

*The next day was the seventh, and on the eighth, Mina pasted into her journal a cutting from the Dailygraph which gave a full account of the way the Russian ship – and it was of course the Demeter – came ashore. It made fascinating reading:*

# THE COFFIN SHIP ARRIVES

*FROM A CORRESPONDENT, WHITBY*

ONE OF THE GREATEST and suddenest storms on record has just been experienced here, with results both strange and unique.

The weather had been somewhat sultry, but not to any degree uncommon in the month of August. The approach of sunset was very beautiful, the wind fell away entirely during the evening, and at midnight there was a dead calm. The only sail noticeable was a foreign schooner with all sails set.

Shortly before ten o'clock the stillness of the air grew quite oppressive, and the silence was so marked that the bleating of a sheep inland or the barking of a dog in the town was distinctly heard. A little after midnight came a strange sound from over the sea, and high overhead the air began to carry a strange, faint, hollow booming.

Then without warning the tempest broke. With a rapidity which seemed incredible, the whole aspect of nature at once became convulsed. The waves rose in growing fury, each over-topping its fellow, till in a very few minutes the lately glassy sea was like a roaring and devouring monster.

The wind roared like thunder, and blew with such force that it was with difficulty that even strong men kept their feet. To add to the difficulties and dangers of the time, masses of sea-fog came drifting inland – white, wet clouds, which swept by in ghostly fashion, so dank and cold that it needed but little effort of imagination to think that the spirits of those lost at sea were touching their living brethren with the clammy hands of death.

At times the mist cleared, and the sea for some distance

could be seen in the glare of the lightning, which now came thick and fast. Some of the scenes thus revealed were of immeasurable grandeur – the sea, running mountains high; here and there a fishing-boat, with a rag of sail, running madly for shelter before the blast; now and again the white wings of a storm-tossed sea-bird.

On the summit of the East Cliff the new searchlight was ready, and in the pauses of the inrushing mist swept the surface of the sea. Once or twice its service was most effective, as when a fishing-boat, with gunwale under water, rushed into the harbour, able, by the guidance of the sheltering light, to avoid the danger of dashing against the piers.

Before long the searchlight discovered some distance away a schooner with all sails set, apparently the same vessel which had been noticed earlier in the evening. The wind had by this time backed to the east, and there was a shudder amongst the watchers on the cliff as they realized the terrible danger in which she now was.

Between her and the port lay the great flat reef on which so many good ships have from time to time suffered, and, with the wind blowing from its present quarter, it would be quite impossible that she should fetch the entrance of the harbour.

It was now nearly the hour of high tide, but the waves were so great that in their troughs the shallows of the shore were almost visible, and the schooner was rushing with such speed that, in the words of one old salt, "she must fetch up somewhere, if it was only in hell."

Then came another rush of sea-fog, greater than any

hitherto — a mass of dank mist, which seemed to close on all things like a grey pall. The rays of the searchlight were kept fixed on the harbour mouth across the East Pier, where the shock was expected, and men waited breathless.

The wind suddenly shifted to the north-east, and the remnant of the sea-fog melted in the blast; and then, *mirabile dictu*, between the piers, leaping from wave to wave as it rushed at headlong speed, swept the strange schooner before the blast, with all sail set, and gained the safety of the harbour.

The searchlight followed her, and a shudder ran through all who saw her, for lashed to the helm was a corpse, with drooping head, which swung horribly to and fro at each motion of the ship. No other form could be seen on the deck at all.

A great awe came on all as they realized that the ship, as if by a miracle, had found the harbour, unsteered save by the hand of a dead man! The schooner, rushing across the harbour, pitched herself on that accumulation of sand and gravel washed by many tides into the south-east corner of the pier.

Strangest of all, the very instant the shore was touched, an immense dog sprang up on deck from below, and running forward, jumped from the bow on the sand. Making straight for the steep cliff where the churchyard hangs over the laneway, it disappeared in the darkness.

# 4

# The Nine Days' Wonder

The Dailygraph's reporter returned to the story in his next edition, dated 9 August, by which time he had decided that it was merely a "mystery of the sea", which would all be forgotten in a few short days.

He reported that the vessel had been carrying a cargo of "great wooden boxes filled with mould". This cargo was consigned to Mr S. F. Billington, a Whitby solicitor, who had already had the goods removed.

Not only was the reporter allowed to read the Demeter's log, but also a most unusual supplement to it, found stuffed into a bottle in the dead captain's pocket – which led him to believe the poor man was insane.

That people had died on board the ship he needed no

*convincing. The question was, did the captain do the killing, while demented? The paper published a digest of the documents, translated from the Russian.*

### LOG OF THE DEMETER: *VARNA TO WHITBY*

On 6 July we finished taking in cargo. At noon set sail. East wind, fresh. Crew, five hands ... two mates, cook, and myself (captain).

On 13 July passed Cape Matapan. Crew dissatisfied about something. Seemed scared, but would not speak out.

On 16 July mate reported in the morning that one of crew, Petrofsky, was missing. Could not account for it. Men more downcast than ever. All said they expected something of the kind, but would not say more than that there was *something* aboard. Mate getting very impatient with them; feared some trouble ahead.

On 17 July, yesterday, one of the men, Olgaren, came to my cabin, and in an awestruck way confided to me that he thought there was a strange man aboard the ship. He said that in his watch he had been sheltering behind the deck-house, as there was a rainstorm, when he saw a tall, thin man, who was not like any of the crew, come up the companion-way, and go along the deck forward, and disappear.

He was in a panic of superstitious fear, and I am afraid the panic may spread. To allay it, I shall today search the entire ship carefully from stem to stern. Men much relieved when search over, and went back to work cheerfully. First mate scowled, but said nothing.

*24 July* – There seems some doom over this ship. Already a hand short, and entering the Bay of Biscay with wild weather ahead, and yet last night another man lost – disappeared. Like the first, he came off his watch and was not seen again. Men all in a panic of fear; sent a round robin, asking to have double watch, as they fear to be alone. Mate angry. Fear there will be some trouble, as either he or the men will do some violence.

*29 July* – Another tragedy. When morning watch came on deck could find no one except steersman. Raised outcry, and all came on deck. Thorough search, but no one found. Are now without second mate, and crew in a panic. Mate and I agreed to go armed henceforth and wait for any sign of cause.

*30 July* – Last night. Rejoiced we are nearing England. Weather fine, all sails set. Retired worn out; slept soundly; awaked by mate telling me that both man of watch and steersman missing. Only self and mate and two hands left to work ship.

*2 August, midnight* – Woke up from few minutes' sleep by hearing a cry. Rushed on deck, and ran against mate. Tells me he heard cry and ran, but no sign of man on watch. One more gone. Lord, help us! We are now in the North Sea, and only

God can guide us in the fog, which seems to move with us; and God seems to have deserted us.

*3 August* – At midnight I went to relieve the man at the wheel, but when I got to it found no one there. The wind was steady, and as we ran before it there was no yawing. I dared not leave it, so shouted for the mate. After a few seconds he rushed up on deck in his flannels. He looked wild-eyed and haggard, and I greatly fear his reason has given way.

He came close to me and whispered hoarsely, with his mouth to my ear, as though fearing the very air might hear: "*It* is here; I know it, now. On the watch last night I saw It, like a man, tall and thin, and ghastly pale. It was in the bows, and looking out. I crept behind It, and gave It my knife; but the knife went through It, empty as the air." And as he spoke he took his knife and drove it savagely into space.

Then he went on: "But It is here, and I'll find It. It is in the hold, perhaps, in one of those boxes. I'll unscrew them one by one and see. You work the helm." And with a warning look and his finger on his lip, he went below.

He is mad, stark, raving mad, and it's no use my trying to stop him. He can't hurt those big boxes: they are invoiced as "clay", and to pull them about is as harmless a thing as he can do. So here I stay, and mind the helm, and write these notes. I can only trust in God and wait till the fog clears.

It is nearly all over now. Just as I was beginning to hope that the mate would come out calmer, there came up the hatchway a sudden, startled scream, which made my blood run cold, and up on the deck he came as if shot from a gun –

a raging madman, with his eyes rolling and his face convulsed with fear.

"Save me! Save me!" he cried, and then looked round on
the blanket of fog. His horror turned to despair, and in a
steady voice he said: "You had better come too, captain,
before it is too late. *He* is there! I know the secret now. The
sea will save me from Him, and it is all that is left!"

Before I could say a word, or move forward to seize him,
he sprang on the bulwark and deliberately threw himself into
the sea.

I suppose I know the secret too, now. It was this madman
who had got rid of the men one by one, and now he has followed them himself. God help me! How am I to account for
all these horrors when I get to port? *When* I get to port! Will
that ever be?

*4 August* – Still fog, which the sunrise cannot pierce. I know
there is sunrise because I am a sailor, why else I know not.
I dared not go below, I dared not leave the helm; so here all
night I stayed, and in the dimness of the night I saw It –
Him! God forgive me, but the mate was right to jump over-
board. It is better to die like a man; to die like a sailor in blue
water no man can object. But I am captain, and I must not
leave my ship. But I shall baffle this fiend or monster, for
I shall tie my hands to the wheel when my strength begins
to fail, and along with them I shall tie that which He – It!
– dare not touch; and then, come good wind or foul, I shall
save my soul, and my honour as a captain.

I am growing weaker, and the night is coming on. If He

can look me in the face again, I may not have time to act... If we are wrecked, mayhap this bottle may be found, and those who find it may understand; if not ... well, then all men shall know that I have been true to my trust. God and the Blessed Virgin and the saints help a poor ignorant soul trying to do his duty...

*Of course, the reporter added dryly, the inquest returned an open verdict. To put it simply, no one had any real idea what might have actually happened. The local people, though, decided the captain was a hero, and it was agreed to bury him in the churchyard on the cliffs.*

*A further minor puzzlement was the dog that "disappeared". As reported, it had jumped off the* Demeter, *but it was never seen again.*

*Other animals seemed to have met it, though. For the newspaper added: "Early this morning a large dog, a half-bred mastiff belonging to a coal merchant close to Tate Hill Pier, was found dead in the roadway opposite its master's yard. It had been fighting, and manifestly had had a savage opponent, for its throat was torn away, and its belly was slit open as if with a savage claw."*

# 5

# A Broken Neck

Although the newspapers did not refer to it again, there is little doubt that the dog from off the ship – mysterious and immense – had some connection or affinity with the churchyard and cemetery. Little doubt either that the Demeter's arrival had some effect on Lucy Westenra.

During the night of the storm, Mina recorded, Lucy was very restless, and got out of bed and dressed herself twice, despite appearing to be still asleep. Each time the careful Mina managed to undress her again, and put her back to bed without waking her.

Two days later they went to the Russian captain's funeral, which they watched from their usual seat above the cemetery, where they had "a lovely view". Every boat in the harbour formed a floating cortège, and the coffin was carried to the graveyard by a guard of honour of sea-captains. Mina wrote it all up in her journal.

\*    \*    \*

# A Broken Neck

## Mina Murray's Journal

*10 August* – Poor Lucy seemed much upset. She was restless and uneasy all the time, and I cannot but think that her dreaming at night is telling on her. There is an additional cause in that poor old Mr Swales was found dead this morning on our seat, his neck being broken.

He had evidently, as the doctor said, fallen back in the seat in some sort of fright, for there was a look of fear and horror on his face that the men said made them shudder. Poor dear old man! Perhaps he had seen Death with his dying eyes!

Lucy is so sweet and sensitive that she feels influences more acutely than other people do. Just now she was quite upset by a little thing which I did not much heed, though I am myself very fond of animals.

One of the men who come up here often to look for the boats was followed by his dog. The dog is always with him. They are both quiet persons, and I never saw the man angry, nor heard the dog bark. During the service the dog would not come to its master, who was on the seat with us, but kept a few yards off, barking and howling.

Its master spoke to it gently, and then harshly, and then angrily; but it would neither come nor cease to make a noise. It was in a sort of fury, with its eyes savage, and all its hair bristling out like a cat's tail when puss is on the warpath.

Finally the man, too, got angry, and jumped down and kicked the dog, and then took it by the scruff of the neck and half dragged and half threw it on the tombstone on which the seat is fixed.

The moment it touched the stone the poor thing became quiet and fell all into a tremble. It did not try to get away, but crouched down, quivering and cowering, and was in such a pitiable state of terror that I tried, though without effect, to comfort it.

Lucy was full of pity, too, but she did not attempt to touch the dog, but looked at it in an agonized sort of way. I greatly fear that she is of too super-sensitive a nature to go through the world without trouble.

She will be dreaming of this tonight, I am sure. The whole agglomeration of things – the ship steered into port by a dead man; his attitude, tied to the wheel with a crucifix and beads; the touching funeral; the dog, now furious and now in terror – will all afford material for her dreams.

*Mina was sadly right. At one o'clock the following morning, she awoke to the beginning of the great disaster. Lucy's bed was empty, and the front door to the house was open...*

# 6
# The Second Seduction

## Mina Murray's Journal

*11 August, 3 a.m.* – No sleep now, so I may as well write. I am too agitated to sleep. We have had such an adventure, such an agonizing experience.

I fell asleep as soon as I had closed my diary... Suddenly I became broad awake, and sat up, with a horrible sense of fear upon me, and of some feeling of emptiness around me.

The room was dark, so I could not see Lucy's bed; I stole across and felt for her. The bed was empty. I lit a match, and found that she was not in the room. The door was shut, but not locked, as I had left it.

I feared to wake her mother, who has been more than usually ill lately, so threw on some clothes and got ready to look for her. "Thank God," I said to myself, "she cannot be far, as she is only in her nightdress."

I ran downstairs and looked in the sitting-room. Not there! Then I looked in all the other rooms of the house, with an ever-growing fear chilling my heart. Finally I came to the hall door and found it open. I took a big, heavy shawl and ran out. The clock was striking one as I was in the Crescent, and there was not a soul in sight.

At the edge of the West Cliff above the pier I looked across the harbour to the East Cliff, in the hope or fear – I don't know which – of seeing Lucy. For a moment or two I could see nothing, as the shadow of a cloud obscured St Mary's Church and all around it. Then as the cloud passed I could see the ruins of the Abbey coming into view; and there, on our favourite seat, a half-reclining figure, snowy white.

The coming of the cloud was too quick for me to see much, for shadow shut down on light almost immediately; but it seemed to me as though something dark stood behind the seat where the white figure shone, and bent over it. What it was, whether man or beast, I could not tell.

I did not wait to catch another glance, but flew down the steep steps to the pier and along by the fish-market to the bridge, which was the only way to reach the East Cliff. I must have gone fast, and yet it seemed to me as if my feet were weighted with lead, and as though every joint in my body were rusty.

When I got almost to the top I could see the seat and the white figure, for I was now close enough to distinguish it even through the spells of shadow. There was undoubtedly something, long and black, bending over the half-reclining white figure. I called in fright, "Lucy! Lucy!" and something raised a head, and from where I was I could see a white face and red, gleaming eyes.

Lucy did not answer, and I ran on to the entrance of the churchyard. As I entered, the church was between me and the seat, and for a minute or so I lost sight of her. When I came in view again the cloud had passed, and the moonlight struck so brilliantly that I could see Lucy half reclining with her head lying over the back of the seat. She was quite alone, and there was not a sign of any living thing about.

When I bent over her I could see that she was still asleep. Her lips were parted, and she was breathing – not softly, as usual with her, but in long, heavy gasps, as though striving to get her lungs full at every breath.

As I came close, she put up her hand in her sleep and

pulled the collar of her nightdress close round her throat. Whilst she did so there came a little shudder through her, as though she felt the cold. I flung the warm shawl over her, and drew the edges tight round her neck, for I dreaded lest she should get some deadly chill from the night air, unclad as she was.

I feared to wake her all at once, so, in order to have my hands free that I might help her, I fastened the shawl at her throat with a big safety pin; but I must have been clumsy in my anxiety and pinched or pricked her with it, for by-and-by, when her breathing became quieter, she put her hand to her throat again and moaned.

When I had her carefully wrapped up I put my shoes on her feet, and then began very gently to wake her. At first she did not respond; but gradually she became more and more uneasy in her sleep, moaning and sighing occasionally.

At last, as time was passing fast, and, for many other reasons, I wished to get her home at once, I shook her more forcibly, till finally she opened her eyes and awoke. She trembled a little, and clung to me; when I told her to come at once with me home she rose without a word, with the obedience of a child.

Fortune favoured us, and we got home without meeting a soul. When we had washed our feet, and had said a prayer of thankfulness together, I tucked her into bed.

Before falling asleep she asked - even implored - me not to

say a word to anyone, even her mother, about her sleep-walking adventure. I hesitated at first to promise; but on thinking of the state of her mother's health, and how the knowledge of such a thing would fret her, I thought it wiser to do so. I hope I did right.

I have locked the door, and the key is tied to my wrist, so perhaps I shall not be again disturbed. Lucy is sleeping soundly; the reflex of the dawn is high and far over the sea...

*Same day, noon* – All goes well. Lucy slept till I woke her. The adventure of the night does not seem to have harmed her; on the contrary, it has benefited her, for she looks better this morning than she has done for weeks.

I was sorry to notice that my clumsiness with the safety pin hurt her. Indeed, it might have been serious, for the skin of her throat was pierced. I must have pinched up a piece of loose skin and have transfixed it, for there are two little red points like pinpricks, and on the band of her nightdress was a drop of blood.

Fortunately it cannot leave a scar, as it is so tiny.

*Same day, night* – We passed a happy day. The air was clear, and the sun bright, and there was a cool breeze. We took our lunch to Mulgrave Woods, Mrs Westenra driving by the road and Lucy and I walking by the cliff-path and joining her at the gate.

I felt a little sad myself, for I could not but feel how

*absolutely* happy it would have been had Jonathan been with me. But there! I must only be patient.

In the evening we strolled in the Casino Terrace, and heard some good music, and went to bed early. Lucy seems more restful than she has been for some time, and fell asleep at once. I shall lock the door and secure the key the same as before, though I do not expect any trouble tonight.

*12 August* – My expectations were wrong, for twice during the night I was wakened by Lucy trying to get out. She seemed, even in her sleep, to be a little impatient at finding the door shut, and went back to bed under a sort of protest. I woke with the dawn, and heard the birds chirping outside of the window.

Lucy woke, too, and, I was glad to see, was even better than on the previous morning. All her old gaiety of manner seemed to have come back, and she came and snuggled in beside me, and told me all about Arthur; I told her how anxious I was about Jonathan, and then she tried to comfort me. Well, she succeeded somewhat, for, though sympathy can't alter facts, it can make them more bearable.

*Unknown to Mina, on the same day that she made that entry a nun in Buda-Pesth was writing her a letter that would not arrive in Whitby for another week.*

*It told how a pale, sick man – clearly delirious – had arrived* in the city some six weeks before, from whither nobody quite knew. He had earlier burst into an eastern station, called Klausenburg, shouting for a ticket home; and "seeing from his violent demeanour that he was English" the station master had given him a ticket to Buda-Pesth, the furthest station on the way, where he had ended up at the hospital of St Joseph and St Mary. He had been suffering from a violent brain fever, Sister Agatha wrote, had very little money left for his care and keep, but had "won all hearts by his sweetness and gentleness", and was being "well cared for". It was Jonathan.

Although the nun had been asked to write to reassure Miss Murray, she added a secret postscript when her patient was asleep. He had had some fearful shock, she reported, and his ravings had been dreadful: of wolves, of poison and of blood – and other worse things that she feared to mention.

Mina, when she received it, set out post-haste to bring him home to England – at the insistence of his employer, Mr Hawkins. That was not until 20 August, however. In the meantime, things in Whitby were getting clearly worse.

# 7

# Unhealing Wounds

## Mina Murray's Journal

13 August – I awoke in the night, and found Lucy sitting up in bed, still asleep, pointing to the window.

I got up quietly, and pulling aside the blind, looked out. It was brilliant moonlight, and the soft effect of the light over the sea and sky – merged together in one great silent mystery – was beautiful beyond words.

Between me and the moonlight flitted a great bat, coming and going in great, whirling circles. Once or twice it came quite close, but was, I suppose, frightened at seeing me, and flitted away across the harbour towards the Abbey.

When I came back from the window Lucy had lain down again, and was sleeping peacefully. She did not stir again all night.

14 August – On the East Cliff, reading and writing all day. Lucy seems to have become as much in love with the spot as

I am, and it is hard to get her away from it when it is time to come home for lunch or tea or dinner.

This afternoon she made a funny remark. We were coming home for dinner, and had come to the top of the steps up from the West Pier and stopped to look at the view, as we generally do.

The setting sun, low down in the sky, was just dropping

behind Kettleness; the red light was thrown over on the East Cliff and the old Abbey, and seemed to bathe everything in a beautiful rosy glow. We were silent for a while, and suddenly Lucy murmured as if to herself, "His red eyes again! They are just the same." It was such an odd expression, coming *apropos* of nothing, that it quite startled me. I slewed round a little, so as to see Lucy well without seeming to stare at her, and saw that she was in a half-dreamy state, with an odd look on her face that I could not quite make out; so I said nothing, but followed her eyes.

She appeared to be looking over at our own seat, whereon was a dark figure seated alone. I was a little startled myself, for it seemed for an instant as if the stranger had great eyes like burning flames; but a second look dispelled the illusion. The red sunlight was shining on the windows of St Mary's Church behind our seat, and as the sun dipped there was just sufficient change to make it appear as if the light moved.

I called Lucy's attention to the peculiar effect, and she became herself with a start, but she looked sad all the same; it may have been that she was thinking of that terrible night up there. We never refer to it; so I said nothing, and we went home to dinner. Lucy had a headache and went early to bed. I saw her asleep, and went out for a little stroll myself.

When coming home – it was then bright moonlight – I threw a glance up at our window, and saw Lucy's head leaning out, lying up against the side of the windowsill. She was fast asleep, and by her was something that looked like a good-sized bird. I ran upstairs, but as I came into the room she was moving back to her bed, fast asleep, and breathing heavily; she was holding her hand to her throat, as though to protect it from the cold.

She looks so sweet as she sleeps; but she is paler than is her wont, and there is a drawn, haggard look under her eyes which I do not like. I fear she is fretting about something. I wish I could find out what it is.

*15 August* – Rose later than usual. Lucy was languid and tired, and slept on after we had been called.

We had a happy surprise at breakfast. Arthur's father is better, and wants the marriage to come off soon. Lucy is full of quiet joy, and her mother is glad and sorry at once. Later on in the day she told me the cause. She is grieved to lose Lucy as her very own, but she is rejoiced that she is soon to have someone to protect her.

Poor dear, sweet lady! She confided to me that she has got her death warrant. She has not told Lucy, and made me promise secrecy; her doctor told her that within a few months, at most, she must die, for her heart is weakening. At any time, even now, a sudden shock would be almost sure to kill her. Ah, we were wise to keep from her the affair of the dreadful night of Lucy's sleepwalking.

\*     \*     \*

*17 August* – No diary for two whole days. I have not had the heart to write. Some sort of shadowy pall seems to be coming over our happiness. No news from Jonathan, and Lucy seems to be growing weaker, whilst her mother's hours are numbering to a close.

I do not understand Lucy's fading away as she is doing. She eats well and sleeps well, and enjoys the fresh air; but all the time the roses in her cheeks are fading, and she gets weaker and more languid day by day; at night I hear her gasping as if for air.

I keep the key of our door always fastened to my wrist at night, but she gets up and walks about the room, and sits at the open window. Last night I found her leaning out when I woke up, and when I tried to wake her I could not; she was in a faint. When I managed to restore her she was as weak as water, and cried silently between long, painful struggles for breath.

When I asked her how she came to be at the window she shook her head and turned away. I trust her feeling ill may not be from that unlucky prick of the safety pin. I looked at her throat just now as she lay asleep, and the tiny wounds seem not to have healed. They are still open, and, if anything, larger than before, and the edges of them are faintly white. They are like little white dots with red centres. Unless they heal within a day or two, I shall insist on the doctor seeing about them.

\*    \*    \*

*A letter was written in Whitby on this date also. It was from S. F. Billington & Son, the solicitors who had taken the consignment of boxes from the grounded Russian schooner* Demeter. *It contained instructions to a London haulage firm.*

*The fifty boxes – after being sent by rail from Whitby to King's Cross station in London – were to be picked up and delivered urgently to the chapel of a house called Carfax, near Purfleet, for which a £10 cheque had been enclosed. Also enclosed was a set of keys, to be left inside the house after the delivery.*

*So on 17 August the chests of foul earth from Castle Dracula moved out of Yorkshire where poor Lucy was. The effect it had on her was extraordinary.*

### Mina Murray's Journal

*18 August* – I am happy today, and write sitting on the seat in the churchyard. Lucy is ever so much better. Last night she slept well all night, and did not disturb me once.

She is in gay spirits and full of life and cheerfulness. All the morbid reticence seems to have passed from her, and she has just reminded me, as if I needed any reminding, of *that* night, and that it was here, on this very seat, I found her asleep. As she told me she tapped playfully with the heel of her boot on the stone slab, like her old self again.

When we got home the fresh breeze had braced her up, and her pale cheeks were really more rosy. Her mother rejoiced when she saw her, and we all spent a very happy evening together.

The very next day, however, Mina received her letter from Sister Agatha, in Buda-Pesth, and by 20 October she had set out to "bring him home". Mr Hawkins – a friend indeed – had suggested further that "it would not be a bad thing" if the couple were to marry out there, while Jonathan was recovering.

So just as things had improved for Lucy, her dear friend went away. Dracula was no longer in Whitby, true – neither as a dog, a bat, nor any other figure, red-eyed and mysterious. And where Dracula was not, it seemed, life could go on, strange illnesses could diminish.

But where was Dracula, exactly? What would his next grim act be – and on whom?

The truth began to emerge very soon...

# 8

# The Madman Awakes

## Dr Seward's Diary

*19 August* - Strange and sudden change in Renfield last night. About eight o'clock he began to get excited and to sniff about as a dog does. The attendant was struck by his manner, and knowing my interest in him, encouraged him to talk. He is usually respectful to the attendant, and at times servile; but tonight, the man tells me, he was quite haughty. All he would say was, "I don't want to talk to you: you don't count now; the Master is at hand."

The attendant thinks it is some sudden form of religious mania which has seized him. If so, we must look out for squalls, for a strong man with homicidal and religious mania at once might be dangerous. The combination is a dreadful one.

At nine o'clock I visited him myself. He became quite quiet, and went and sat on the edge of his bed resignedly, and looked into space with lacklustre eyes.

I thought I would find out if his apathy were real or only

assumed, and tried to lead him to talk of his pets, a theme which had never failed to excite his attention. At first he made no reply, but at length said testily, "Bother them all! I don't care a pin about them."

"What?" I said. "You don't mean to tell me you don't care about spiders?"

To this he answered enigmatically, "The bride-maidens rejoice the eyes that wait the coming of the bride; but when the bride draweth nigh, then the maidens shine not to the eyes that are filled."

He would not explain himself, but remained obstinately seated on his bed all the time I remained with him.

I am weary tonight and low in spirits. I cannot but think of Lucy, and how different things might have been. If I don't sleep at once – chloral, the modern Morpheus! I must be careful not to let it grow into a habit. No, I shall take none tonight! I have thought of Lucy, and I shall not dishonour her by mixing the two. If need be, tonight shall be sleepless...

Glad I made the resolution; gladder that I kept to it. I had lain tossing about, and had heard the clock strike only twice, when the night-watchman came to me to say that Renfield had escaped. I threw on my clothes and ran down at once; my patient is too dangerous a person to be roaming about.

The attendant was waiting for me. He said he had seen him not ten minutes before, seemingly asleep in his bed, when he had looked through the observation-trap in the door. His attention was called by the sound of the window being wrenched out. He ran back and saw his feet disappear through the window, and had at once sent up for me.

The attendant told me the patient had gone to the left and had taken a straight line, so I ran as quickly as I could. As I got through the belt of trees I saw a white figure scale the high wall which separates our grounds from those of the deserted house.

I ran back at once, and told the watchman to get three or four men immediately and follow me into the grounds of Carfax, in case our friend might be dangerous. I got a ladder myself, and crossing the wall, dropped down on the other side. I could see Renfield's figure just disappearing behind the angle of the house, so I ran after him.

On the far side of the house I found him pressed close against the old iron-bound oak door of the chapel. He was talking, apparently to someone, but I could see that he did not take note of anything around him, and so ventured to draw nearer to him. I heard him say, "I am here to do Your bidding, Master. I am Your slave, and You will reward me, for I shall be faithful. I have worshipped You long and afar off. Now that You are near, I await Your commands."

When we closed in on him he fought like a tiger. He is immensely strong, and he was more like a wild beast than a man. I never saw a lunatic in such a paroxysm of rage before; and I hope I shall not again. He is safe now at any rate, chained to the wall in the padded room. His cries are at times awful, but the silences that follow are more deadly still, for he means murder in every turn and movement.

Just now he spoke coherent words for the first time: "I shall be patient, Master. It is coming - coming - coming!"

So I took the hint, and came too. I was too excited to sleep, but this diary has quieted me, and I feel I shall get some sleep tonight.

*For three days and nights, Seward recorded later, Renfield followed a pattern – "violent all day, then quiet from moonrise to sunrise" – which the doctor longed to know the reason for. Finally he deliberately left the madman's padded room unlocked. After one false start, Renfield did escape, as planned. Now he could be followed...*

## Dr Seward's Diary

23 *August* - Another night adventure. Again he went into the grounds of the deserted house, and we found him in the same place, pressed against the old chapel door. When he saw me he became furious, and had not the attendants seized him in time, he would have tried to kill me.

As we were holding him a strange thing happened. He suddenly redoubled his efforts, and then as suddenly grew calm. I looked round instinctively, but could see nothing.

Then I caught the patient's eye and followed it, but could

trace nothing as it looked into
the moonlit sky except a big bat,
which was flapping its silent and ghostly way to the west.

Bats usually wheel and flit about, but this one seemed to go straight on, as if it knew where it was bound for or had some intention of its own. The patient grew calmer every instant, and presently said, "You needn't tie me; I shall go quietly!" Without trouble we came back to the house. I feel there is something ominous in his calm, and shall not forget this night...

*The very next day, Lucy Westenra began a diary. She was at home in Hillingham with her mother now, the Whitby holiday over. Her husband-to-be was a frequent visitor, but her friend and confidante, Mina, was abroad in Buda-Pesth. For Lucy, things were rapidly becoming unbearable.*

# 9

# Desperate Measures

## Lucy Westenra's Diary

*Hillingham, 24 August* – I must imitate Mina, and keep writing things down. Then we can have long talks when we do meet. I wonder when it will be. I wish she were with me again, for I feel so unhappy.

Last night I seemed to be dreaming again just as I was at Whitby. Perhaps it is the change of air, or getting home again. It is all dark and horrid to me, for I can remember nothing; but I am full of vague fear, and I feel so weak and worn out.

When Arthur came to lunch he looked quite grieved when he saw me, and I hadn't the spirit to try to be cheerful. I wonder if I could sleep in mother's room tonight. I shall make an excuse to try.

*25 August* – Another bad night. Mother did not seem to take to my proposal. She seems not too well herself, and doubtless she fears to worry me. I tried to keep awake, and succeeded for a while; but when the clock struck twelve it waked me from a doze, so I must have been falling asleep.

There was a sort of scratching or flapping at the window, but I did not mind it, and as I remember no more, I suppose I must then have fallen asleep. More bad dreams. I wish I could remember them.

This morning I am horribly weak. My face is ghastly pale, and my throat pains me. It must be something wrong with my lungs, for I don't seem ever to get air enough. I shall try to cheer up when Arthur comes, or else I know he will be miserable to see me so.

*Only six days later, Arthur Holmwood wrote to his old friend Jack Seward about her. Considering that Lucy had rejected the doctor's marriage offer, but that he still loved her and Holmwood knew it, his letter argues a worry about her state of health that bordered on the desperate.*

*Albemarle Hotel, 31 August*

My dear Jack,

I want you to do me a favour. Lucy is ill; that is, she has no special disease, but she looks awful, and is getting worse every day. I have asked her if there is any cause; I do not dare to ask her mother, for to disturb the poor lady's mind about her daughter in her present state of health would be fatal. Mrs Westenra has confided to me that her doom is spoken – disease of the heart – though poor Lucy does not know it yet.

I am sure that there is something preying on my dear girl's mind. I am most distracted when I think of her; to look at her gives me a pang. I told her I should ask you to see her, and though she demurred at first – I know why, old fellow – she finally consented.

It will be a painful task for you, I know, old friend, but it is for *her* sake, and I must not hesitate to ask, or you to act. You are to come to lunch at Hillingham tomorrow, two o'clock, so as not to arouse any suspicion in Mrs Westenra, and after lunch Lucy will take an opportunity of being alone with you. I shall come in for tea, and we can go away together; I am filled with anxiety, and want to consult with you alone as soon as I can after you have seen her. Do not fail!

ARTHUR

*In the event, Holmwood was called away to see his ailing father, whose condition had got worse. Dr Seward went to Hillingham alone. He wrote his findings in a letter to his friend.*

*2 September*

My dear old fellow,

With regard to Miss Westenra's health, I hasten to let you know at once that in my opinion there is not any functional disturbance or any malady that I know of. At the same time, I am not by any means satisfied with her appearance; she is woefully different from what she was when I saw her last.

I found Miss Westenra in seemingly gay spirits. We lunched, and as we all exerted ourselves to be cheerful, we got, as some kind of reward for our labours, some real cheerfulness amongst us. Then Mrs Westenra went to lie down, and Lucy was left with me.

As soon as the door was closed, however, the mask fell from her face, and she sank down into a chair with a great sigh, and hid her eyes with her hand. In physical matters I was quite satisfied that there is no need for anxiety; but as there must be a cause somewhere, I have come to the conclusion that it must be something mental.

I am in doubt, and so have done the best thing I know of; I have written to my old friend and master, Professor Van Helsing, of Amsterdam, who knows as much about obscure diseases as anyone in the world. He is a philosopher and a metaphysician, and one of the most advanced scientists of his day; and he has, I believe, an absolutely open mind.

I tell you these facts that you may know why I have such confidence in him. I have asked him to come at once.

Yours always,

JOHN SEWARD

## LETTER FROM ABRAHAM VAN HELSING

*The doctor hardly pulled his punches, but he was perhaps less than fully frank about his former teacher's field of expertise. The Dutchman worked in many disciplines, some of them bordering on the secret and bizarre. Everything about him, indeed – including his grasp of English – was unusual. And modest he was not... He replied immediately, by return of post.*

*2 September*

My good Friend,

Have rooms for me at the Great Eastern Hotel, so that I may be near to hand, and please it so arrange that we may see the young lady not too late on tomorrow, for it is likely that I may have to return here that night. But if need be I shall come again in three days, and stay longer if it must. Till then goodbye, my friend John.

VAN HELSING

# 10

# A Terrible Change for the Worse

Despite her weakening condition, Lucy Westenra was trying very hard to put her bravest face on things. On 30 August – just one day before Arthur Holmwood sought such urgent help from Seward – she wrote a letter to Mina Murray that was full of hope ... and lies.

It was addressed not to Miss Murray, though, but to Mrs Harker, and was in response to Mina's news from Buda-Pesth. She had written that she had found her "dear one, oh, so thin and pale and weak-looking ... only a wreck of himself", but capable of setting an instant date for the wedding ceremony, inside the hospital where he lay. They had, in fact, been married with Jonathan propped up with pillows to say "I will".

"Then he took my hand in his," wrote Mina, "and oh, Lucy, it was the first time he took his wife's hand, and said that it was the dearest thing in all the wide world."

*Mina told Lucy that Jonathan had given her a notebook, his shorthand diary of his time away, and invited her to read it – only if she wanted to – to "share his ignorance", because he truly did not know if the things he half remembered were "real or the dreaming of a madman". Mina sealed it up, as a "visible sign for us all our lives that we trusted each other", and said that she would only open it "for his own dear sake or for the sake of some stern duty."*

*She finished her letter with hopes for Lucy's own future as a wife – to be as happy, in fact, as she was now as Mrs Harker...*

*Mina was happy – but poor Lucy was living on the edge of a nightmare. Despite her worry and despair, though, she wrote Mina this bubbling reply. Whether deliberately, or from sad confusion, she even dated it from Whitby. She was, in fact, at Hillingham.*

*Whitby, 30 August*

My dearest Mina,

Oceans of love and millions of kisses, and may you soon be in your own home with your husband. I wish you could be coming home soon enough to stay with us here. This strong air would soon restore Jonathan; it has quite restored me. I have an appetite like a cormorant, am full of life, and sleep well.

You will be glad to know that I have quite given up walking in my sleep. I think I have not stirred out of my bed for a week, that is when I once got into it at night. Arthur says I am getting fat.

By the way, I forgot to tell you that Arthur is here. We have such walks and drives, and rides, and rowing, and tennis, and fishing together; and I love him more than ever.

He *tells me* that he loves me more, but I doubt that, for at first he told me that he couldn't love me more than he did then. But this is nonsense. There he is, calling to me. So no more just at present from your loving
Lucy

P.S. Mother sends her love. She seems better, poor dear.
P.P.S. We are to be married on 28 September.

*After Van Helsing's visit, Dr Seward was trying brave faces too, when he wrote to Arthur Holmwood. Dated four days after Lucy's, though, his letter was not half as cheerful.*

*3 September*

My dear Art,

Van Helsing has come and gone. He came on with me to Hillingham, and found that, by Lucy's discretion, her mother was lunching out, so that we were alone with her.

Van Helsing made a very careful examination of the patient. He is to report to me, and I shall advise you, for of course I was not present all the time.

He is, I fear, much concerned. When I told him of our friendship and how you trust to me in the matter, he looked grave, and said, "I have made careful examination, but there is no functional cause.

"And yet there is cause; there is always cause for everything. I must go back home and think. You must send to me the telegram every day; and if there be cause I shall come again.

"The disease – for not to be all well is a disease – interest me, and the sweet young dear, she interest me too. She charm me, and for her, if not for you or disease, I come."

He would not say a word more, even when we were alone. And so now, Art, you know all I know. I shall keep stern watch.

I trust your poor father is rallying. It must be a terrible thing to you, my dear old fellow, to be placed in such a position between two people who are both so dear to you.

I know your idea of duty to your father, and you are right to stick to it; but, if need be, I shall send you word to come at once to Lucy; so do not be over-anxious unless you hear from me.

*The next day, while waiting for developments, Seward busied himself with Renfield once again. His mood swings, by now, were becoming almost regular, it seemed, and the doctor began to think he could see a pattern. Just before noon the patient would grow restless, then so violent it took all the attendants' strength to hold him. Then, in five minutes or so, he would sink into "a sort of melancholy", which could last for hours.*

*By five o'clock he would be "as happy and contented as he used to be", and catching flies and eating them again – then at sunset he would become violent and have to be restrained.*

*On one of these occasions, the doctor wrote, the madman "looked very sad, and said in a sort of far-away voice, 'All over! All over! He has deserted me. No hope for me now unless I do it for myself!'"*

*So – paroxysms at noon and sunset, a tragic sense of loss, a feeling of having been deserted. Seward sensed that he was close to understanding. Unfortunately, however, there were other problems on his mind. He kept up his daily telegrams about Lucy.*

TELEGRAM, SEWARD, LONDON, TO VAN HELSING, AMSTERDAM

*4 September* – PATIENT STILL BETTER TODAY.

TELEGRAM, SEWARD, LONDON, TO VAN HELSING, AMSTERDAM

*5 September* – PATIENT GREATLY IMPROVED. GOOD APPETITE; SLEEPS NATURALLY; GOOD SPIRITS; COLOUR COMING BACK.

*6 September* – TERRIBLE CHANGE FOR THE WORSE. COME AT ONCE; DO NOT LOSE AN HOUR. I HOLD OVER TELEGRAM TO HOLMWOOD TILL HAVE SEEN YOU.

# The First Infusion

## Dr Seward's Diary

*7 September* – The first thing Van Helsing said to me when we met at Liverpool Street was, "Have you said anything to our young friend the lover of her?"

"No," I said. "I waited till I had seen you, as I said in my telegram. I wrote him a letter simply telling him that you were coming, as Miss Westenra was not so well, and that I should let him know if need be."

"Right, my friend," he said, "quite right! Better he not know as yet; perhaps he shall never know."

When we were shown in, Mrs Westenra met us. She was alarmed, but I laid down a rule that she should not be present with Lucy or think of her illness more than was absolutely required. She assented so readily that I saw the hand of Nature fighting for life.

Van Helsing and I were shown up to Lucy's room. If I was shocked when I saw her yesterday, I was horrified when I saw her today. She was ghastly, chalkily pale; the red seemed to have gone even from her lips and gums, and the bones of her face stood out prominently; her breathing was painful to see or hear.

Van Helsing's face grew set as marble, and his eyebrows converged till they almost touched over his nose. Lucy lay motionless, and did not seem to have strength to speak, so for a while we were all silent.

Then Van Helsing beckoned to me, and we went gently out of the room. The instant we had closed the door he stepped quickly along the passage to the next door, which was open. Then he pulled me quickly in with him and closed the door.

"My God!" he said. "This is dreadful. There is no time to be lost. She will die for sheer want of blood to keep the heart's action as it should be. There must be a transfusion at once. Is it you or me?"

"I am younger and stronger, Professor. It must be me."

"Then get ready at once. I will bring up my bag. I am prepared."

I went downstairs with him, and as we were going there

was a knock at the hall door. When we reached the hall the maid had just opened the door, and Arthur was stepping quickly in. He rushed up to me, saying in an eager whisper, "Jack, I was so anxious. I read between the lines of your letter, and have been in an agony. The dad was better, so I ran down here to see for myself. Is not that gentleman Dr Van Helsing? I am so thankful to you, sir, for coming."

When first the Professor's eye had lit upon him he had been angry at any interruption at such a time; but now, as he took in his stalwart proportions and recognized the strong young manhood which seemed to emanate from him, his eyes gleamed.

"Sir, you have come in time. You are the lover of our dear miss. She is bad, very, very bad. Nay, my child, do not go like that." For he suddenly grew pale and sat down in a chair almost fainting. "You are to help her. You can do more than any that live, and your courage is your best help."

"What can I do?" asked Arthur hoarsely. "Tell me, and I shall do it. My life is hers, and I would give the last drop of blood in my body for her. What shall I do?"

Van Helsing slapped him on the shoulder.

"Come!" he said. "You are a man, and it is a man we want. Young miss wants blood, and blood she must have or die. My friend John and I have consulted; and we are about to perform what we call transfusion - to transfer from full veins of one to the empty veins which pine for him."

"If you only knew how gladly I would die for her you would understand—"

He stopped, with a sort of choke in his voice.

"Good boy!" said Van Helsing. "In the not-so-far-off you will be happy that you have done all for her you love.

"Come now and be silent. You shall kiss her once before it is done, but then you must go; and you must leave at my sign. Say no word to Madame; you know how it is with her! There must be no shock. Come!"

We all went up to Lucy's room. Arthur by direction remained outside. Lucy turned her head and looked at us, but said nothing. She was not asleep, but she was simply too weak to make the effort. Her eyes spoke to us; that was all.

Van Helsing took some things from his bag and laid them on a little table out of sight. Then he mixed a narcotic, and coming over to the bed, said cheerily, "Now, little miss, here is your medicine. Drink it off, like a good child. See, I lift you so that to swallow is easy. Yes."

It astonished me how long the drug took to act. The time seemed endless until sleep began to flicker in her eyelids. At last, however, the narcotic began to manifest its potency; and she fell into a deep sleep. When the Professor was satisfied he called Arthur into the room, and bade him strip off his coat.

Then he added, "You may take that one little kiss whiles I bring over the table. Friend John, help to me!" So neither of us looked whilst he bent over her.

Then with swiftness, but with absolute method, Van Helsing performed the operation. As the transfusion went on something like life seemed to come back to poor Lucy's cheeks, and through Arthur's growing pallor the joy of his face seemed absolutely to shine.

When all was over I could see how much Arthur was weakened. I dressed the wound and took his arm to bring him away, when Van Helsing spoke without turning round, "The brave lover, I think, deserve another kiss, which he shall have presently." And as he had now finished his operation, he adjusted the pillow to the patient's head.

As he did so the narrow black velvet band which she seems always to wear round her throat, buckled with an old diamond buckle which her lover had given her, was dragged a little up, and showed a red mark on her throat. Arthur did not notice it, but I could hear the deep hiss of indrawn breath which is one of Van Helsing's ways of betraying emotion.

He said nothing at the moment, but turned to me, saying, "Now take down our brave young lover, give him of the port wine, and let him lie down a while. He must then go home and rest, sleep much and eat much, that he may be recruited of what he has so given to his love.

"Hold! A moment. I may take it, sir, that you are anxious of result. Then bring it with you that in all ways the operation is successful. You have saved her life this time, and you can go home and rest easy in mind that all that can be is. I shall tell her all when she is well; she shall love you none the less for what you have done. Goodbye."

When Arthur had gone I went back to the room. Lucy was sleeping gently, but her breathing was stronger; I could see the counterpane move as her breast heaved. By the bedside sat Van Helsing, looking at her intently. The velvet band again covered the red mark. I asked the Professor in a whisper, "What do you make of that mark on her throat?"

"What do you make of it?"

"I have not seen it yet," I answered, and then and there proceeded to loose the band. Just over the external jugular vein there were two punctures, not large, but not wholesome-looking. It occurred to me that this wound might be the means of loss of blood, but I abandoned the idea as soon as formed, for such a thing could not be. The whole bed would have been drenched to a scarlet with the blood which the girl must have lost to leave such a pallor as she had before the transfusion.

"Well?" said Van Helsing.

"Well," said I, "I can make nothing of it."

The Professor stood up. "I must go back to Amsterdam tonight," he said. "There are books and things there which I want. You must remain here all the night, and you must not let your sight pass from her."

"Shall I have a nurse?" I asked.

"We are the best nurses, you and I. You keep watch all night; see that she is well fed, and that nothing disturbs her.

You must not sleep. I shall be back as soon as possible. And then we may begin."

"May begin?" I said. "What on earth do you mean?"

"We shall see!" he answered as he hurried out. He came back a moment later and put his head inside the door, and said, with a warning finger held up, "Remember, she is your charge. If you leave her, and harm befall, you shall not sleep easy hereafter!"

*Dr Seward did sit up all night at Lucy's bedside, and apparently the next night, too (his diary dates, as usual, are ambiguous). Before the first time he had a conversation with her, in which Lucy revealed her dread of sleeping because of things that happened in the night. "But, my dear girl" (wrote Jack Seward), "you may sleep tonight. I promise you that if I see any evidence of bad dreams I will wake you at once."*

"You will? Oh, will you really? How good you are to me. Then I will sleep!" And almost at the word she gave a deep sigh of relief, and sank back, asleep.

*On 9 September Van Helsing suggested in a telegram from Amsterdam that Seward should attend his charge at Hillingham again, and the doctor – although exhausted – went along. This time, however, he allowed Lucy's womanly compassion (as he saw it) to get the better of his judgement and instructions.*

\*      \*      \*

## Dr Seward's Diary

9 September – I was pretty tired and worn out when I got to Hillingham. Lucy was up and in cheerful spirits. When she shook hands with me she looked sharply in my face and said, "No sitting up tonight for you. You are worn out. I am quite well again; indeed, I am; and if there is to be any sitting up, it is I who will sit up with you." Then Lucy took me upstairs, and showed me a room next her own, where a cosy fire was burning.

"Now," she said, "you must stay here. I shall leave this door open and my door too. You can lie on the sofa, for I know that nothing would induce any of you doctors to go to bed whilst there is a patient above the horizon. If I want anything I shall call out, and you can come to me at once."

I could not but acquiesce, for I was "dog-tired", and could not have sat up had I tried. So, on her renewing her promise to call me if she should want anything, I lay on the sofa, and forgot all about everything.

*Lucy, as she confided in her diary, felt "so happy". She was sleeping marvellously, with "that dear, good Dr Seward close at hand and within call."*

*Van Helsing was due from Amsterdam in the morning, too, and everybody was being wonderful to her. The last words that she wrote were these: "Thank God! Goodnight, Arthur."*

## 12

# A Wreath of Garlic

### Dr Seward's Diary

*10 September* – I was conscious of the Professor's hand on my head, and started awake all in a second. That is one of the things that we learn in an asylum, at any rate.

"And how is our patient?"

"Well, when I left her, or rather when she left me," I answered.

"Come, let us see," he said. And together we went into the room.

The blind was down, and I went over to raise it gently, whilst Van Helsing stepped, with his soft, cat-like tread, over to the bed.

As I raised the blind, and the morning sunlight flooded the room, I heard the Professor's low hiss of inspiration, and knowing its rarity, a deadly fear shot through my heart.

As I passed over he moved back, and his exclamation of horror, *"Gott in Himmel!"* needed no enforcement from his agonized face. He raised his hand and pointed to the bed, and his iron face was drawn and ashen white. I felt my knees begin to tremble.

There on the bed, seemingly in a swoon, lay poor Lucy, more horribly white and wan-looking than ever. Even the lips were white, and the gums seemed to have shrunken back from the teeth, as we sometimes see in a corpse after a prolonged illness.

Van Helsing raised his foot to stamp in anger, but the instinct of his life and all the long years of habit stood to him, and he put it down again softly.

"Quick!" he said. "Bring the brandy."

I flew to the dining-room, and returned with the decanter. He wetted the poor white lips with it, and together we rubbed palm and wrist and heart. He felt her heart, and after a few moments of agonizing suspense said, "It is not too late. It beats, though but feebly. All our work is undone; we must begin again. There is no young Arthur here now; I have to call on you yourself this time, friend John."

As he spoke, he was dipping into his bag and producing the instruments for transfusion; I had taken off my coat and rolled up my shirt-sleeve. There was no possibility of an opiate just at present, and no need of one; and so, without a moment's delay, we began the operation.

After a time, I could see a faint tinge of colour steal back into the pallid cheeks and lips. No man knows, till he experiences it, what it is to feel his own life-blood drawn away into the veins of the woman he loves.

The Professor watched me critically.

"That will do," he said.

"Already?" I remonstrated. "You took a great deal more from Art."

To which he smiled a sad sort of smile as he replied, "He is her lover, her *fiancé*."

When we stopped the operation, he attended to Lucy, whilst I applied digital pressure to my own incision. By-and-by he bound up my wound, and sent me downstairs to get a glass of wine for myself. As I was leaving the room, he came after me, and half whispered, "Mind, nothing must be said of this. If our young lover should turn up unexpected, as before, no word to him. It would at once frighten him and enjealous him, too. There must be none. So!"

Lucy slept well into the day; and when she woke she was fairly well and strong, though not nearly so much so as the day before. When Van Helsing had seen her, he went out for a walk, leaving me in charge, with strict injunctions that I was not to leave her for a moment. I could hear his voice in the hall, asking the way to the nearest telegraph office.

Lucy chatted with me freely, and seemed quite unconscious that anything had happened. I tried to keep her amused and interested. When her mother came up to see her, she did not seem to notice any change whatever, but said to me gratefully, "We owe you so much, Dr Seward, for all you have done, but you really must now take care not to overwork yourself. You are looking pale yourself. You want a wife to nurse and look after you a bit; that you do!"

As she spoke, Lucy turned crimson, though it was only momentarily, for her poor wasted veins could not stand for long such an unwonted drain to the head. As she turned imploring eyes on me, I smiled and nodded, and laid my finger on my lips; with a sigh, she sank back amid her pillows.

Van Helsing returned in a couple of hours, and presently said to me, "Now you go home, and eat much and drink enough. Make yourself strong. I stay here tonight, and I shall sit up with little miss myself.

"You and I must watch the case, and we must have none other to know. I have grave reasons. No, do not ask them; think what you will. Do not fear to think even the most not-probable. Goodnight."

★　　★　　★

*11 September* – This afternoon I went over to Hillingham. Found Van Helsing in excellent spirits, and Lucy much better. Shortly after I had arrived, a big parcel from abroad came for the Professor. He opened it – and showed a great bundle of white flowers.

"These are for you, Miss Lucy," he said.

"For me? Oh, Dr Van Helsing!"

"Yes, my dear, but not for you to play with. These are medicines. I put him in your window, I make pretty wreath, and hang him round your neck, so that you sleep well. Oh yes! They, like the lotus flower, make your trouble forgotten."

Whilst he was speaking, Lucy had been examining the flowers and smelling them. Now she threw them down, saying, with half-laughter and half-disgust, "Oh, Professor, I believe you are only putting up a joke on me. Why, these flowers are only common garlic."

To my surprise, Van Helsing rose up and said with all his sternness, his iron jaw set and his bushy eyebrows meeting, "No trifling with me! I never jest! There is grim purpose in all I do; and I warn you that you do not thwart me. Take care, for the sake of others if not for your own."

Then seeing poor Lucy scared, as she might well be, he went on more gently, "Oh, little miss, my dear, do not fear me. I only do for your good; but there is much virtue to you in those so common flower. See, I place them myself in your room. I make myself the wreath that you are to wear. Sit still awhile.

"Come with me, friend John, and you shall help me deck the room with my garlic, which is all the way from Haarlem, where my friend Vanderpool raise herb in his glass-houses all the year. I had to telegraph yesterday, or they would not have been here."

We went into the room, taking the flowers with us. First the Professor fastened up the windows and latched them securely; next, taking a handful, he rubbed them all over the sashes, as though to ensure that every whiff of air that might get in would be laden with the garlic smell. Then with the wisp he rubbed all over the jamb of the door, above, below, and at each side, and round the fireplace in the same way.

It all seemed grotesque to me, and presently I said, "Well, Professor, I know you always have a reason for what you do, but this certainly puzzles me. It is well we have no sceptic here, or he would say that you were working some spell to keep out an evil spirit."

"Perhaps I am!" he answered quietly as he began to make the wreath which Lucy was to wear round her neck.

We then waited whilst Lucy made her toilet for the night, and when she was in bed he came and himself fixed the wreath of garlic round her neck. The last words he said to her were, "Take care you do not disturb it; and even if the room feel close, do not tonight open the window or the door."

"I promise," said Lucy, "and thank you both a thousand

times for all your kindness to me! Oh, what have I done to be blessed with such friends?"

As we left the house, Van Helsing said, "Tonight I can sleep in peace, and sleep I want – two nights of travel, much reading in the day between, and much anxiety on the day to follow, and a night to sit up, without to wink. Tomorrow in the morning early you call for me, and we come together to see our pretty miss, so much more strong for my 'spell' which I have work. Ho, ho!"

He seemed so confident that I, remembering my own confidence two nights before and with the baneful result, felt awe and vague terror. It must have been my weakness that made me hesitate to tell it to my friend, but I felt it all the more, like unshed tears.

## Lucy Westenra's Diary

*11 September* – How good they all are to me. I quite love that dear Dr Van Helsing. I wonder why he was so anxious about these flowers. He positively frightened me, he was so fierce.

And yet he must have been right, for I feel comfort from them already. Somehow, I do not dread being alone, and I can go to sleep without fear. I shall not mind any flapping outside the window. I never liked garlic before, but tonight it is delightful! There is peace in its smell; I feel sleep coming already. Goodnight, everybody.

# 13

## Lucy Alone

*Although both Lucy and Jack Seward were startled at Van Helsing's sudden loss of temper over the garlic, he was in fact being most restrained. Unprepared as yet to voice his deep suspicions, even to his former favourite pupil, he thought he knew the awful truth of what was happening. Garlic was a charm to ward off vampires – and a vampire, he feared, was sucking Lucy's blood.*

*If he was right, her survival, he knew, was already in some doubt. If the attacks continued, the very gates of hell would open up before her. To save her life would be impossible; to save her ever-lasting soul would involve rituals of unutterable vileness. Her head would have to be hacked off, her body pierced with a wooden stake. Van Helsing snapped, and then apologized. Perhaps a better plan would have been to be more frank. Jack Seward's "unshed tears", likewise, would have been much better shed.*

*They left her there that evening, and went off to their beds. Next morning they were at the front door early. And for a short time everything seemed well...*

## Dr Seward's Diary

*12 September* – Let all be put down exactly. Van Helsing and I arrived at Hillingham at eight o'clock. It was a lovely morning; the bright sunshine and all the fresh feeling of early autumn seemed like the completion of nature's annual work.

When we entered we met Mrs Westenra coming out of the morning room. She greeted us warmly and said, "You will be glad to know that Lucy is better. The dear child is still asleep. I looked into her room and saw her, but did not go in, lest I should disturb her."

The Professor smiled, and looked quite jubilant. He rubbed his hands together, and said, "Aha! I thought I had diagnosed the case. My treatment is working."

To which she answered, "You must not take all the credit to yourself, doctor. Lucy's state this morning is due in part to me."

"How do you mean, ma'am?" asked the Professor.

"Well, I was anxious about the dear child in the night, and went into her room. She was sleeping soundly – so soundly that even my coming did not wake her. But the room was awfully stuffy. There were a lot of those horrible, strong-smelling flowers about everywhere, and she had actually a bunch of them round her neck.

"I feared that the heavy odour would be too much for the dear child in her weak state, so I took them all away and opened a bit of the window to let in a little fresh air. You will be pleased with her, I am sure."

She moved off into her boudoir, where she usually break-fasted early. As she had spoken, I watched the Professor's face, and saw it turn ashen grey. He had been able to retain his self-command whilst the poor lady was present, for he knew her state and how mischievous a shock would be; he actually smiled on her as he held open the door for her to pass into her room.

But the instant she had disappeared he pulled me, sud-denly and forcibly, into the dining-room and closed the door.

Then, for the first time in my life, I saw Van Helsing break down. He raised his hands over his head in a sort of mute despair, and then beat his palms together in a helpless way; finally he sat down on a chair, and putting his hands before his face, began to sob, with loud, dry sobs that seemed to come from the very racking of his heart.

Then he raised his arms again, as though appealing to the whole universe. "God! God! God!" he said. "What have we done, what has this poor thing done, that we are so sore beset? This poor mother, all unknowing, does such thing as lose her daughter body and soul; and we must not tell her, we must not even warn her, or she die, then both die. Oh, how we are beset! How are all the powers of the devils against us!"

Suddenly he jumped to his feet. "Come," he said, "come, we must see and act. Devils or no devils, or all the devils at once, it matters not; we fight him all the same." He went to the hall door for his bag, and together we went up to Lucy's room.

Once again I drew up the blind, whilst Van Helsing went towards the bed. This time he did not start as he looked on the poor face with the same awful, waxen pallor as before. He wore a look of stern sadness and infinite pity.

Without a word he went and locked the door, and then began to set out on the little table the instruments for yet another operation of transfusion of blood. I had begun to take off my coat, but he stopped me with a warning hand.

"No!" he said. "Today you must operate. I shall provide. You are weakened already." As he spoke he took off his coat and rolled up his shirt-sleeve.

Again the operation; again the narcotic; again some return of colour to the ashy cheeks, and the regular breathing of healthy sleep. This time I watched whilst Van Helsing re-cruited himself and rested.

Presently he took an opportunity of telling Mrs Westenra that she must not remove anything from Lucy's room without consulting him; that the flowers were of medicinal value, and that the breathing of their odour was a part of the system of cure. Then he took over the care of the case himself, saying that he would watch this night and the next and would send me word when to come.

After another hour Lucy waked from her sleep, fresh and bright and seemingly not much the worse for her terrible ordeal.

What does it all mean? I am beginning to wonder if my

long habit of life amongst the insane is beginning to tell upon my own brain.

*However hard the learning of their lessons, the two men now knew what they could or could not do. From that day forward, Lucy was always in their sight as soon as night fell. And she thrived on it.*

### Lucy Westenra's Diary

*17 September* - Four days and nights of peace. I am getting so strong again that I hardly know myself. It is as if I had passed through some long nightmare, and had just awakened to see the beautiful sunshine and feel the fresh air of the morning around me.

Bad dreaming seems to have passed away; the noises that used to frighten me out of my wits - the flapping against the windows, the distant voices which commanded me to do I know not what - have all ceased. I go to bed now without any fear of sleep. I do not even try to keep awake.

Tonight Dr Van Helsing is going away, as he has to be for a day in Amsterdam. But I need not be watched; I am well enough to be left alone.

*Lucy's lack of awareness sounds alarming, but Van Helsing had absolutely no intention of leaving her unguarded. On his way to Amsterdam he "sent word" as promised – a telegram – to*

Dr Seward, at Carfax. It was despatched from Antwerp, and the telegraph service in those days – British and foreign – was excellent. Nothing could go wrong.

Except that Van Helsing was not English. The telegram was addressed to SEWARD, CARFAX, with no county stipulated. It reached Jack Seward on 18 September, with a message from the Telegraph Offices attached: "Sent to Carfax, Sussex, as no county given; delivered late by twenty-two hours." The telegram read as follows:

17 September – DO NOT FAIL TO BE AT HILLINGHAM TONIGHT. VERY IMPORTANT; DO NOT FAIL. SHALL BE WITH YOU AS SOON AS POSSIBLE.

Seward read it on the eighteenth, and its effect on him may be easily imagined. Lucy had spent all night alone again, and he knew only too well what could be wrought upon her helpless body in a night. As he entered in his diary: "Surely there is some horrible doom hanging over us that every possible accident should thwart us in all we try to do."

Lucy, as she waited helpless for the last attack, the night before he wrote this, must have felt more certain of that awful doom. Abandoned, she was forced to write an account of it, which she tucked into the bosom of her nightdress in the hope it would be read when she was gone...

\*   \*   \*

*Memorandum Left by Lucy Westenra*

*17 September, night* – I write this and leave it to be seen, so that no one may by any chance get into any trouble through me. This is an exact record of what took place tonight. I feel I am dying of weakness, and have barely strength to write, but it must be done if I die in the doing.

I went to bed as usual, taking care that the flowers were placed as Dr Van Helsing directed, and soon fell asleep.

I was waked by the flapping at the window, which now I know so well. I was not afraid, but I did wish that Dr Seward was in the next room – as Dr Van Helsing said he would be – so that I might have called him. I tried to go to sleep, but could not.

Then outside in the shrubbery I heard a sort of howl like a dog's, but more fierce and deeper. I went to the window and looked out, but could see nothing, except a big bat, which had evidently been buffeting its wings against the window.

Presently the door opened, and mother came in, and sat by me. She said to me even more sweetly and softly than her wont, "I was uneasy about you, darling, and came in to see that you were all right."

I feared she might catch cold sitting there, and asked her to come in and sleep with me. As she lay there in my arms, and I in hers, the flapping and buffeting came to

the window again. She was startled and a little frightened, and cried out, "What is that?"

I tried to pacify her, and at last succeeded, and she lay
quiet; but I could hear her poor dear heart still beating
terribly.

After a while there was the low howl again out in the
shrubbery, and shortly after there was a crash at the
window, and a lot of broken glass was hurled on the floor.

The window blind blew back with the wind that
rushed in, and in the aperture of the broken panes there
was the head of a great, gaunt grey wolf.

Mother cried out in a fright, and struggled up into
a sitting posture, and clutched wildly at anything that
would help her. Amongst other things, she clutched the
wreath of flowers that Dr Van Helsing insisted on my
wearing round my neck, and tore it away from me.

For a second or two she sat up, pointing at the wolf,
and there was a strange and horrible gurgling in her
throat; then she fell over, as if struck with lightning, and
her head hit my forehead and made me dizzy for
a moment or two. The room and all round seemed to
spin round.

I kept my eyes fixed on the window, but the wolf
drew his head back, and a whole myriad of little specks
seemed to come blowing in through the broken window,
and wheeling and circling round.

I tried to stir, but there was some spell upon me, and dear mother's poor body, which seemed to grow cold already – for her dear heart had ceased to beat – weighed me down; and I remembered no more for a while.

The time did not seem long, but very, very awful, till I recovered consciousness again. Somewhere near, a passing bell was tolling; the dogs all round the neighbour-hood were howling; and in our shrubbery, seemingly just outside, a nightingale was singing. I was dazed and stupid with pain and terror and weakness, but the sound of the nightingale seemed like the voice of my dead mother come back to comfort me.

The sounds seemed to have awakened the maids, too, for I could hear their bare feet pattering outside my door. I called to them, and they came in, and when they saw what had happened, and what it was that lay over me on the bed, they screamed out.

The wind rushed in through the broken window, and the door slammed to. They lifted off the body of my dear mother, and laid her, covered up with a sheet, on the bed after I had got up. They were all so frightened and nervous that I directed them to go to the dining-room and have each a glass of wine.

The door flew open for an instant and closed again. The maids shrieked, and then went in a body to the dining-room; and I laid what flowers I had on my dear mother's breast. When they were there I remembered what Dr Van Helsing had told me, but I didn't like to remove them, and besides, I would have some of the ser-vants to sit up with me now.

I was surprised that the maids did not come back. I called them, but got no answer, so I went to the dining-room to look for them. They all four lay helpless on the floor, breathing heavily. The decanter of sherry was on the table half full, but there was a queer, acrid smell about, of laudanum.

What am I to do? What am I to do? I am back in the room with mother. I cannot leave her, and I am alone, save for the sleeping servants, whom someone has drugged.

Alone with the dead! I dare not go out, for I can hear the low howl of the wolf through the broken window. The air seems full of specks, floating and circling in the draught from the window, and the lights burn blue and dim.

What am I to do? God shield me from harm this night! I shall hide this paper in my breast, where they shall find it when they come to lay me out. My dear mother gone! It is time that I go too. Goodbye, dear Arthur, if I should not survive this night. God keep you, dear, and God help me!

# 14

# A Stand-up Fight with Death

Doctor Seward, when he realized the terrible mistake next morning, raced to Hillingham as fast as horse-drawn cab could take him. But no servants responded to his frantic knocking, and every door was barred and bolted. Van Helsing came hurrying up the driveway from a hired carriage shortly afterwards, and when he saw the doctor, who should have been inside all night, he gasped.

"Just arrived?" he said. "How is she?" Realization began to dawn... "Did you not get my telegram?"

Seward explained, and the two men gained entry by cutting through some window bars with a surgical saw from the Dutchman's leather bag. They found a scene of horror: four servant women drugged unconscious, and upstairs, at Lucy's bedroom door, the utmost silence. When they entered, both men had "white faces and trembling hands".

## Dr Seward's Diary

How shall I describe what we saw? On the bed lay two women, Lucy and her mother. The latter lay farthest in, and she was covered with a white sheet, the edge of which had been blown back by the draught, showing the drawn, white face, with a look of terror fixed upon it.

By her side lay Lucy, with face white and still more drawn. The flowers which had been round her neck we found upon her mother's bosom, and her throat was bare, showing the two little wounds which we had noticed before, but looking horribly white and mangled.

Without a word the Professor bent over the bed, his head almost touching poor Lucy's breast; then he gave a quick turn of his head, as of one who listens, and leaping to his feet, he cried out to me, "It is not yet too late! Quick! Quick! Bring the brandy!"

I flew downstairs and returned with it, taking care to smell and taste it, lest it, too, were drugged like the decanter of sherry which I found on the table. He rubbed the brandy on her lips and gums and on her wrists and the palms of her hands. He said to me, "I can do this, you go wake those maids. Flick them in the face with a wet towel, and flick them hard. Make them get heat and fire and a warm bath. This poor soul is nearly as cold as that beside her. She will need be heated before we can do anything more."

I went at once, and found little difficulty in waking the

women. As remembrance came back to them they cried and sobbed in a hysterical manner. I was stern with them, however, and would not let them talk. I told them that one life was bad enough to lose, and that if they delayed they would sacrifice Miss Lucy. So, sobbing and crying, they went about their way, half-clad as they were, and prepared fire and water.

Fortunately, the kitchen and boiler fires were still alive, and there was no lack of hot water. We got a bath, and carried Lucy out as she was and placed her in it. Whilst we were busy chafing her limbs there was a knock at the hall door. One of the maids ran off, hurried on some more clothes, and opened it.

Then she returned and whispered to us that there was a gentleman who had come with a message from Mr Holmwood. I bade her simply tell him that he must wait, for we could see no one now. She went away, and, engrossed with our work, I clean forgot all about him.

I never saw in all my experience the Professor work in such deadly earnest. I knew – as he knew – that it was a stand-up fight with death, and in a pause told him so. He answered me in a way that I did not understand, but with the sternest look that his face could wear, "If that were all, I would stop here where we are now, and let her fade away into peace, for I see no light in life over her horizon." He went on with his work with, if possible, renewed and more frenzied vigour.

Presently we both began to be conscious that the heat was beginning to be of some effect. Lucy's heart beat a trifle more audibly to the stethoscope, and her lungs had a perceptible movement. Van Helsing's face almost beamed, and as we lifted her from the bath and rolled her in a hot sheet to dry her, he said to me, "The first gain is ours! Check to the King!"

We took Lucy into another room, which had by now been prepared, and laid her in bed and forced a few drops of brandy down her throat. I noticed that Van Helsing tied a soft silk handkerchief round her throat. She was still unconscious, and was quite as bad as we had ever seen her.

Van Helsing called in one of the women, and told her to stay with her and not to take her eyes off her till we returned, and then beckoned me out of the room.

"We must consult as to what is to be done," he said as we descended the stairs. In the hall he opened the dining-room door, and we passed in, he closing the door carefully behind him. The room was dimly dark. It was, however, light enough for our purposes. Van Helsing was evidently torturing his mind about something, so I waited for an instant, and he spoke. "What are we to do now? Where are we to turn for help? We must have another transfusion of blood, and that soon, or that poor girl's life won't be worth an hour's purchase. You are exhausted already; I am exhausted too. I fear to trust those women, even if they would have courage to submit. What are we to do for someone who will open his veins for her?"

"What's the matter with me, anyhow?"

# A Stand-up Fight with Death

The voice came from the sofa across the room, and Van Helsing started angrily at the sound. But his face softened and a glad look came into his eyes as I cried out, "Quincey Morris!" and rushed towards him with outstretched hands.

"What brought you here?" I cried as our hands met.

"I guess Art is the cause."

He handed me a telegram:

HAVE NOT HEARD FROM SEWARD FOR THREE DAYS, AND AM TERRIBLY ANXIOUS. CANNOT LEAVE. FATHER STILL IN SAME CONDITION. SEND ME WORD HOW LUCY IS. DO NOT DELAY – HOLMWOOD.

"I think I came just in the nick of time. You know you have only to tell me what to do."

Van Helsing strode forward and took his hand, looking him straight in the eyes as he said, "A brave man's blood is the best thing on this earth when a woman is in trouble. You're a man, and no mistake. Well, the devil may work against us for all he's worth, but God sends us men when we want them."

Once again we went through that ghastly operation. I have not the heart to go through with the details. Lucy had got a terrible shock, and it told on her more than before, for though plenty of blood went into her veins, her body did not respond to the treatment as well as on the other occasions. Her struggle back into life was something frightful to see and hear.

However, the action of both heart and lungs improved, and Van Helsing made a subcutaneous injection of morphia, as before, and with good effect. Her faint became a profound slumber.

The Professor watched whilst I went downstairs with Quincey Morris, and told the cook to get ready a good breakfast. Then I went back to the room where Lucy now was.

When I came softly in, I found Van Helsing with a sheet or two of notepaper in his hand. He had evidently read it, and was thinking it over as he sat with his hand to his brow. There was a look of grim satisfaction in his face, as of one who has had a doubt solved. He handed me the paper saying only, "It dropped from Lucy's breast."

When I had read it, I stood looking at the Professor, and after a pause asked him, "In God's name, what does it all mean? Was she, or is she, mad; or what sort of horrible danger is it?" I was so bewildered that I did not know what to say more. Van Helsing put out his hand and took the paper.

"Do not trouble about it now. Forget it for the present. You shall know and understand it all in good time; but it will be later."

When I got back Quincey was waiting for me. He said, "Jack Seward, I don't want to shove myself in anywhere where I've no right to be; but this is no ordinary case. The Dutchman said, that time you two came into the room, that you must have *another* transfusion of blood, and that both you and he were exhausted; I guess Art was in it too. Jack, if you may tell me without betraying confidence, Arthur was the first; is not that so?"

"That's so."

"And how long has this been going on?"

"About ten days."

"Ten days! Then I guess, Jack Seward, that that poor pretty creature that we all love has had put into her veins within that time the blood of four strong men. Man alive, her whole body wouldn't hold it."

Then, coming close to me, he spoke in a fierce half-whisper: "What took it out?"

I shook my head. "That," I said, "is the crux. Van Helsing is simply frantic about it, and I am at my wits' end. I can't even hazard a guess. There has been a series of little circumstances which have thrown out all our calculations as to Lucy being properly watched. But these shall not occur again. Here we stay until all be well - or ill."

Quincey held out his hand.

"Count me in," he said. "You and the Dutchman will tell me what to do, and I'll do it."

When she woke late in the afternoon, Lucy's eye lit on Van Helsing and on me too, and gladdened.

Then she looked round the room, and seeing where she was, shuddered; she gave a loud cry, and put her poor thin hands before her pale face. We both understood what that meant – that she had realized to the full her mother's death; so we tried what we could to comfort her.

19 September – All last night she slept fitfully, being always afraid to sleep and something weaker when she woke from it. The Professor and I took it in turns to watch, and we never left her for a moment unattended.

When the day came, its searching light showed the ravages in poor Lucy's strength. She was hardly able to turn her head, and the little nourishment which she could take seemed to do her no good. At times she slept, and both Van Helsing and I noticed the difference in her, between sleeping and waking.

Whilst asleep she looked stronger, although more haggard, and her breathing was softer; her open mouth showed the pale gums drawn back from the teeth, which thus looked positively longer and sharper than usual; when she woke, the softness of her eyes evidently changed the expression, for she looked her own self, although a dying one.

In the afternoon she asked for Arthur, and we telegraphed

for him. Quincey went off to meet him at the station.

When he arrived it was nearly six o'clock, and the sun was setting full and warm, and the red light streamed in through the window and gave more colour to the pale cheeks. When he saw her, Arthur was simply choking with emotion, and none of us could speak.

In the hours that had passed, the fits of sleep, or the comatose condition that passed for it, had grown more frequent, so that the pauses when conversation was possible were shortened. Arthur's presence, however, seemed to act as a stimulant; she rallied a little, and spoke to him more brightly than she had done since we arrived. He too pulled himself together, and spoke as cheerily as he could, so that the best was made of everything.

It is now nearly one o'clock, and he and Van Helsing are sitting with her. I am to relieve them in a quarter of an hour, and I am entering this on Lucy's phonograph. Until six o'clock they are to try to rest. I fear that tomorrow will end our watching, for the shock has been too great; the poor child cannot rally. God help us all.

# 15

# The Gaping Grave

*In the world outside the tragic house at Hillingham, life went on of course. On 17 September, as the final assault on Lucy was slowly building up, Mina Harker was writing to her friend from Exeter with some quite fantastic news. It concerned Mr Hawkins, Jonathan's employer and friend.*

My dearest Lucy,

It seems *an age* since I heard from you, or indeed since I wrote. You will pardon me, I know, for all my faults when you have read my news.

Well, I got my husband back all right; when we arrived at Exeter there was a carriage waiting for us, and in it, though he had an attack of gout, Mr Hawkins. He took us to his own house, where there were rooms for us all nice and comfortable, and we dined together. After dinner Mr Hawkins said, "My dears, I want to drink your health and prosperity; and may every blessing attend you both. I know you both from children, and have, with love and pride, seen you grow up.

"Now I want you to make your home here with me. I have left to me neither chick nor child; all are gone, and in my will I have left you everything." I cried, Lucy dear, as Jonathan and the old man clasped hands. Our evening was a very, very happy one.

So here we are, installed in this beautiful old house, and from both my bedroom and drawing-room I can see the great elms of the cathedral close, with their great black stems standing out against the old yellow stone of the cathedral. I am busy, I need not tell you, arranging things and housekeeping. Jonathan and Mr Hawkins are busy all day; for, now that Jonathan is a partner, Mr Hawkins wants to tell him all about the clients.

How is your dear mother getting on? I wish I could run up to town for a day or two to see you, dear, but I dare not go yet, with so much on my shoulders; and Jonathan wants looking after still.

He is beginning to put some flesh on his bones again, but he was terribly weakened by the long illness; even now he sometimes starts out of his sleep in a sudden way and awakes all trembling until I can coax him back to his usual placidity. However, thank God, these occasions grow less frequent as the days go on, and they will in time pass away altogether, I trust.

And now I have told you my news, let me ask yours. When are you to be married, and where, and who is to perform the ceremony, and what are you to wear, and is it to be a public or a private wedding?

Tell me all about it, dear; tell me all about everything, for there is nothing which interests you which will not be dear to me. Goodbye, my dearest Lucy, and all blessings on you.

Yours,

MINA HARKER

*Lucy, sadly, never saw the letter.*

*In Carfax, also, things were moving on. Before rushing to Hillingham, John Seward, the conscientious doctor, had put a man in charge with even more qualifications than he had – a Patrick Hennessey, MD. Hennessey sent him constant reports, the first one referring to Renfield, who had had "another outbreak".*

*It appeared that two men from a London haulage firm – Dr Hennessey took down their names and details – had arrived to remove some "great wooden boxes" from the old chapel in the property next door. Renfield had got wind of it, and had hurled abuse at them from his window when they had come to the asylum for directions.*

*Later, as the men had returned along the road, their wagon* now laden with the heavy boxes, Renfield had escaped. He had set upon the carters and tried to kill them, it seemed – until attendants, Hennessey and the men themselves had managed to subdue him with a straitjacket.

"I'll frustrate them!" Renfield had shouted. "They shan't rob me! They shan't murder me by inches! I'll fight for my Lord and Master!"

He had ended up, as so frequently, in a padded cell.

Neither Hennessey (of course) nor Dr Seward realized the implications of this event, and Van Helsing was not told of it till much later. What it meant, in fact, was that Dracula had arranged for his coffin "homes" to be taken off elsewhere.

Renfield, not guessing that it was "his Master's" own decision, assumed that he was being robbed – of his reason for existence. Without the coffins ... his Master would be gone.


The very day after her most happy letter, Mina Harker was forced to write another, very sad. Good Mr Hawkins, having done his last great kindness to them, had suddenly died.

Although it meant that they were now well off, Jonathan was left to bear the running of the firm alone, which Mina feared he no longer had the mental strength to do. The funeral was to be in London, she added, where Mr Hawkins' father was already buried, and they would call on Lucy if they had the time, but all was very stressed and stressful.

"Forgive me, dear," wrote Mina, with unknowing irony, "if

*I worry you with my troubles in the midst of your own happiness; but, Lucy dear, I must tell someone, for the strain tries me."*

This letter, too, remained unopened by Miss Westenra. At Hillingham the strains were more than trying. To add to them, news had come that Arthur's father, Lord Godalming, had died at last.

## Dr Seward's Diary

*20 September* – Only resolution and habit can let me make an entry tonight. I am too miserable, too low-spirited, too sick of the world and all in it, including life itself, that I would not care if I heard this moment the flapping of the wings of the angel of death. And he has been flapping those grim wings to some purpose of late – Lucy's mother and Arthur's father, and now... Let me get on with my work.

I duly relieved Van Helsing in his watch over Lucy. We wanted Arthur to go to rest also, but he refused at first. It was only when I told him that we should want him to help us during the day, and that we must not all break down for want of rest, lest Lucy should suffer, that he agreed to go.

Van Helsing was very kind to him. "Come, my child," he said; "come with me. You are sick and weak, and have had much sorrow and much mental pain.

"Come to the drawing-room, where there is a big fire, and there are two sofas. You shall lie on one, and I on the other, and our sympathy will be comfort to each other, even though we do not speak, and even if we sleep."

Arthur went off with him, casting back a longing look on Lucy's face. She lay quite still, and I looked round the room to see that all was as it should be.

I could see that the Professor had carried out his purpose of using the garlic; the whole of the window-sashes reeked with it, and round Lucy's neck, over the silk handkerchief which Van Helsing made her keep on, was a rough chaplet of the same odorous flowers.

Lucy was breathing somewhat stertorously, and her face was at its worst, for the open mouth showed the pale gums. Her teeth, in the dim, uncertain light, seemed longer and sharper than they had been in the morning. In particular, by some trick of the light, the canine teeth looked longer and sharper than the rest.

I sat down by her, and presently she moved uneasily. At the same moment there came a sort of dull flapping or buffeting at the window. I went over to it softly, and peeped out by the corner of the blind. There was a full moonlight, and I could see that the noise was made by a great bat, which wheeled round, and every now and again struck the window with its wings.

When I came back to my seat I found that Lucy had moved slightly, and had torn away the garlic flowers from her throat. I replaced them as well as I could, and sat watching her.

Presently she woke, and I gave her food, as Van Helsing had prescribed. She took but a little, and that languidly. There did not seem to be with her now the unconscious struggle for life and strength that had hitherto so marked her illness.

At six o'clock Van Helsing came to relieve me. Arthur had then fallen into a doze, and he mercifully let him sleep on. When he saw Lucy's face I could hear the hissing indraw of his breath, and he said to me in a sharp whisper, "Draw up the blind. I want light!"

Then he bent down, and, with his face almost touching Lucy's, examined her carefully. He removed the flowers and lifted the silk handkerchief from her throat. As he did so he started back, and I could hear his ejaculation, *"Mein Gott!"* as it was smothered in his throat. I bent over and looked too, and as I noticed, some queer chill came over me.

The wounds on the throat had absolutely disappeared.

For fully five minutes Van Helsing stood looking at her, with his face at its sternest. Then he turned to me and said calmly, "She is dying. It will not be long now. Wake that poor boy, and let him come and see the last; he trusts us, and we have promised him."

I went to the dining-room and waked him. He was dazed for a moment, but I took him by the hand and raised him up. "Come," I said, "my dear old fellow, summon all your fortitude; it will be best and easiest for *her.*"

When we came into Lucy's room I could see that Van

Helsing had, with his usual forethought, been putting matters straight and making everything look as pleasing as possible. He had even brushed Lucy's hair, so that it lay on the pillow in its usual sunny ripples. She opened her eyes, and whispered softly, "Arthur! Oh, my love, I am so glad you have come!"

He was stooping to kiss her, when Van Helsing motioned him back. "No," he whispered, "not yet! Hold her hand; it will comfort her more."

So Arthur took her hand and knelt beside her, and she looked her best, with all the soft lines matching the angelic beauty of her eyes. Then gradually her eyes closed, and she sank to sleep. For a little bit her breast heaved softly, and her breath came and went like a tired child's.

And then insensibly there came the strange change which I had noticed in the night. Her breathing grew stertorous, the mouth opened, and the pale gums, drawn back, made the teeth look longer and sharper than ever. In a sort of sleep-waking, vague, unconscious way she opened her eyes, which were now dull and hard at once, and said in a soft, voluptuous voice, such as I had never heard from her lips, "Arthur! Kiss me!"

Arthur bent eagerly over to kiss her; but at that instant Van Helsing, who, like me, had been startled by her voice, swooped upon him, and catching him by the neck with both hands, dragged him back with a fury of strength which I never thought he could have possessed, and actually hurled him almost across the room.

"Not for your life!" he said. "Not for your living soul and hers!" And he stood between them like a lion at bay.

Arthur was so taken aback that he did not for a moment know what to do or say; and before any impulse of violence could seize him he realized the place and the occasion, and stood silent, waiting.

I kept my eyes fixed on Lucy, as did Van Helsing, and we saw a spasm as of rage flit like a shadow over her face; the sharp teeth champed together. Then her eyes closed, and she breathed heavily.

Very shortly after, she opened her eyes in all their softness, and putting out her poor pale, thin hand, took Van Helsing's great brown one; drawing it close to her, she kissed it. "My true friend," she said, in a faint voice, but with untellable pathos. "My true friend, and his! Oh, guard him, and give me peace!"

"I swear it!" said he solemnly, kneeling beside her and holding up his hand, as one who registers an oath. Then he turned to Arthur, and said to him, "Come, my child, take her hand in yours, and kiss her on the forehead, and only once."

Their eyes met instead of their lips; and so they parted.

Lucy's eyes closed; and Van Helsing, who had been watching closely, took Arthur's arm, and drew him away.

And then Lucy's breathing became stertorous again, and all at once it ceased.

"It is all over," said Van Helsing. "She is dead!"

I took Arthur by the arm, and led him away to the drawing-room, where he sat down, and covered his face with his hands, sobbing in a way that nearly broke me down to see.

I went back to the room, and found Van Helsing looking at poor Lucy, and his face was sterner than ever.

Some change had come over her body. Death had given back part of her beauty, for her brow and cheeks had recovered some of their flowing lines; even the lips had lost their deadly pallor. It was as if the blood, no longer needed for the working of the heart, had gone to make the harshness of death as little rude as might be.

I stood beside Van Helsing, and said, "Ah well, poor girl, there is peace for her at last. It is the end!"

He turned to me, and said with grave solemnity, "Not so; alas! Not so. It is only the beginning!"

When I asked him what he meant, he only shook his head and answered, "Wait and see."

# Book Three

# THE EVIL SPREADS

# 1

# Burying the Dead

Lucy's mother, Mr Hawkins, Arthur's father – and now Lucy. Death was in the air; death was rampant. But only Van Helsing, so far, was prepared to face the truth. Despite all the Professor's hinting, despite all the strange and terrible events, Jack Seward seemed incapable of understanding that they had slipped into a world of evil.

Perhaps he was being blind, perhaps merely rational, but he claimed, in his diary, to believe that it was now over – that Lucy's death was indeed the end, whatever the Dutchman might say or hint. His journal entries, however, have a tendency to skirt around reality. His stubbornness, in fighting it, was monumental.

Faced with Arthur Holmwood's state of bereaved collapse, for instance, he took refuge in the famous English "stiff upper lip" – and suggested they go and view the corpse. When his friend's sobs had subsided, he led him to the bedroom where Lucy lay in state.

## Dr Seward's Diary

God! How beautiful she was. Every hour seemed to be enhancing her loveliness. It frightened and amazed me somewhat; and as for Arthur, he fell a-trembling, and finally was shaken with doubt as with an ague.

At last, after a long pause, he said to me in a faint whisper, "Jack, is she really dead?"

*Seward assured him that she was, although earlier he had been similarly shocked. Indeed, he had written, "I could not believe my eyes that I was looking at a corpse."*

*Even after Lucy and her mother had been buried in the family tomb, moods and emotions among the friends were raw and fragile.*

*Van Helsing talked rationally to Holmwood about the pain of Lucy's death, and asked permission to read all her letters and papers to help throw light on certain things. But later, alone with Seward, he had a fit of wild hysterics – which he insisted was merely his "sense of humour asserting itself under very terrible conditions."*

*Seward, reasonably, asked what place a sense of humour had in such sad circumstances, but Van Helsing's answer was enigmatic. If Seward understood, he said, he would pity him most of all.*

*"Why?" asked Seward.*

*"Because I know!" came the reply.*

*And it was left at that; Jack Seward merely dropped the*

*subject. His modern-day equivalent, in psychiatry, might have said that he, the doctor, was deeply in denial.*

*Jonathan Harker also suffered some kind of a collapse – after Mr Hawkins' funeral, which took place in another part of London.*

*After the ceremony, he and Mina caught a bus to Hyde Park Corner, then took a stroll down Rotten Row – just like real tourists.*

*Mina's attention was taken by "a very beautiful girl, in a big cartwheel hat" waiting in a carriage outside a shop, when suddenly (as she related in her journal):* I felt Jonathan clutch my arm so tight that he hurt me, and he said under his breath, "My God!"

He was very pale, and his eyes seemed bulging out as, half in terror and half in amazement, he gazed at a tall, thin man, with a beaky nose and black moustache and pointed beard, who was also observing the pretty girl.

He was looking at her so hard that he did not see either of us, and so I had a good view of him. His face was not a good face; it was hard, and cruel, and sensual, and his big white teeth, that looked all the whiter because his lips were so red, were pointed like an animal's.

Jonathan kept staring at him, till I was afraid he would notice. I feared he might take it ill, he looked so fierce and nasty. I asked Jonathan why he was disturbed, and he answered: "It is the man himself! I believe it is the Count, but he has grown young. My God, if this be so! Oh, my God! My God!"

He was distressing himself so much that I drew him away quietly, and he, holding my arm, came easily. We walked a little further, and then went in and sat for a while in the Green Park. It was a hot day for autumn, and there was a comfortable seat in a shady place. After a few minutes' staring at nothing, Jonathan's eyes closed, and he went quietly into a sleep. In about twenty minutes he woke up, and said to me quite cheerfully, "Why, Mina, have I been asleep? Oh, do forgive me for being so rude. Come, and we'll have a cup of tea somewhere."

He had evidently forgotten all about the dark stranger, as in his illness he had forgotten all that this episode had reminded him of. I don't like this. I must not ask him, for fear I shall do more harm than good; but I must somehow learn the facts of his journey abroad.

The time is come, I fear, when I must open that parcel and know what is written. Oh, Jonathan, you will, I know, forgive me if I do wrong, but it is for your own dear sake.

*Later* – A sad homecoming in every way – the house empty of the dear soul who was so good to us; Jonathan still pale and dizzy; and now a telegram from Van Helsing, whoever he may be:

YOU WILL BE GRIEVED TO HEAR THAT MRS WESTENRA DIED FIVE DAYS AGO, AND THAT LUCY DIED THE DAY BEFORE YESTERDAY. THEY WERE BOTH BURIED TODAY.

Oh, what a wealth of sorrow in a few words! Poor Mrs Westenra! Poor Lucy! Gone, gone, never to return to us! And poor, poor Arthur, to have lost such sweetness out of his life! God help us all to bear our troubles.

*Whether some of those troubles – especially Jonathan's – had been real or merely wild imaginings, Mina was not yet sure. Like Dr Seward, though, she was confident, despite her husband's hallucinations in Rotten Row, of one thing: all the ghastliness was in the past.*

*Seward expressed it in his journal thus:* And now we are all scattered; and for many a long day loneliness will sit over our roofs with brooding wings. Lucy lies in the tomb of her kin, a lordly death-house in a lonely churchyard, so I can finish this diary. Here at the end, ere I go back to take up the thread of my life-work, I say sadly and without hope, FINIS.

*Finis. Finished. The end. The entry screams of desperate, misplaced optimism. It was dated 22 September.*

*And back in Exeter the next day, Jonathan having gone out on some complicated legal work, Mina Harker locked herself into her room and settled down to read his secret shorthand journal...*

# 2

## Mina on Her Knees

### Mina Harker's Journal

*24 September* - I hadn't the heart to write last night; that terrible record of Jonathan's upset me so. Poor dear! How he must have suffered. I wonder if there is any truth in it at all. Did he get his brain fever, and then write all those terrible things; or had he some cause for it all? I suppose I shall never know, for I dare not open the subject to him...

And yet that man we saw! He seemed quite certain of him... Poor fellow! I suppose it was the funeral upset him and sent his mind back on some train of thought.

I shall get my typewriter this very hour and begin transcribing. If ever Jonathan quite gets over the nervousness he may want to tell me of it all, and I can ask him questions and find out things, and see how I may comfort him.

*Next day, however, Mina received a letter from Van Helsing. He told her that he had read all Lucy's papers – by permission of her fiancé, Arthur (Lord Godalming, as he now was following his father's death) – and asked if he could come to Exeter, to talk.*

*Mina assumed, naturally, that it was about Lucy's condition, or her "sleepwalking", that he wanted information, although she hoped that he could also "throw some light upon Jonathan's sad experience." Her husband was still away, but she replied – by telegram – immediately.*

*25 September* – COME TODAY BY QUARTER PAST TEN TRAIN IF YOU CAN CATCH IT. CAN SEE YOU ANY TIME YOU CALL. WILHELMINA HARKER.

*Van Helsing, the old charmer, arrived at half past two, and flattered her as hard and as carefully as he had always flattered Lucy Westenra. She was instantly impressed, and handed him a typescript of the diary of her times with Lucy, and the strange events in Whitby. He read it while she ordered luncheon from her kitchen staff (the middle classes all had cooks and servants in those days), and when they met again he was "ablaze with excitement".*

*He asked her about Jonathan – "Is he quite well? Is all that fever gone, and is he strong and hearty?" – and soon Mina had told him of her worries. She broke down as she talked of the London trip and the strange encounter in the park.*

*"He thought he saw someone who recalled something terrible,"* *she told Van Helsing, "something which led to his brain fever." She added in her journal:* And here the whole thing seemed to over-

whelm me in a rush. The pity of Jonathan, the horror which he experienced, the whole fearful mystery of his diary, and the fear that has been brooding over me ever since, all came in a tumult.

I suppose I was hysterical, for I threw myself on my knees and held up my hands to him, and implored him to make my husband well again. I began to fear that he would think me a weak fool, and Jonathan a madman, and I hesitated to go on. But he was so sweet and kind, and he had promised to help, and I trusted him, so I said, "Dr Van Helsing, what I have to tell you is so queer that you must not laugh at me or at my husband. I have been since yesterday in a sort of fever of doubt; you must be kind to me, and not think me foolish that I have even half believed some very strange things."

*Van Helsing reassured her. The reason he had come to see her was because of things that "make one doubt if they be mad or sane." Mina, gratefully, told him of her husband's journal, and he took it to his hotel to read.*

*Within hours – by six o'clock that night – he had sent a note.*

Dear Madam Mina,

I have read your husband's so wonderful diary. You may sleep without doubt. Strange and terrible as it is, it is *true*! I will pledge my life on it.

Yours the most faithful,

ABRAHAM VAN HELSING

*Mina replied immediately, by hand. She thanked him profusely, and said the weight had been lifted from her mind. She invited him to breakfast the next morning, when Jonathan would also be at home, and told him there was a London train at 10.30, by which time they would have finished talking.*

*"What an awful thing," she added, "if that man, that monster, be really in London! I fear to think..."*

## Jonathan Harker's Journal

26 September – I thought never to write in this diary again, but the time has come. When I got home last night Mina had supper ready, and when we had supped she told me of Van Helsing's visit, and of her having given him the two diaries copied out, and of how anxious she has been about me.

She showed me in the doctor's letter that all I wrote down was true. We sat late, and talked it all over. Mina is dressing, and I shall call at the hotel in a few minutes and bring him over...

He was, I think, surprised to see me. When I introduced myself, he took me by the shoulder, and turned my face round to the light, and said, after a sharp scrutiny, "But Madam Mina told me you were ill, that you had had a shock."

It was so funny to hear my wife called "Madam Mina" by this kindly, strong-faced old man. I smiled, and said, "I *was* ill, I *have* had a shock; but you have cured me already."

"And how?"

"By your letter to Mina last night. I was in doubt, and then everything took a hue of unreality, and I did not know what to trust, even the evidence of my own senses. Doctor, you don't know what it is to doubt everything, even yourself. No, you don't; you couldn't with eyebrows like yours."

He seemed pleased, and laughed as he said, "So! You are physiognomist. I learn more here with each hour. I am with so much pleasure coming to you to breakfast; and, oh, sir, you will pardon praise from an old man, but you are blessed in your wife."

I would listen to him go on praising Mina for a day, so I simply nodded and stood silent.

"And now," he said, "may I ask you for some more help? I have a great task to do, and at the beginning it is to know. Can you tell me what went before your going to Transylvania? Later on I may ask more help, and of a different kind; but at first this will do."

"Look here, sir," I said, "I am with you heart and soul. As you go by the 10.30 train, you will not have time to read them; but I shall get the bundle of papers. You can take them with you and read them in the train."

*After they had breakfasted, Jonathan saw Van Helsing to the station. As a courtesy he bought him newspapers for the journey, in case he finished the bundle of information about the trip to Castle Dracula. As they chatted at the carriage window,* waiting for the train to start, the Dutchman leafed idly through them.

Suddenly, to Jonathan's consternation, he seemed to spot something – and grew quite white. He read intently, groaning to himself, "Mein Gott! Mein Gott! So soon! So soon!"

Just then the whistle blew, and the train moved off. Recovering himself, Van Helsing leaned from the window and waved his hand, calling out, "Love to Madam Mina; I shall write so soon as ever I can."

The paper was the Westminster Gazette, and the story was about the abduction of some Hampstead children, singly, over several nights. None of them, it seemed, had been badly hurt – but some of them had marks upon their necks. When asked, they had said it was "the bloofer lady...".

The plague, it seemed, was breaking out again.

# 3

# The Empty Coffin

*In his asylum next to Carfax, John Seward was working rather miserably when Van Helsing confronted him with reality once more. Again he was stubborn in the face of it. It was, he noted in his diary, less than a week since he had written "Finis" on the whole affair, and his energies were now all channelled into getting over Lucy's death.*

*"Truly," he wrote, "there is no such thing as finality."*

## Dr Seward's Diary

26 September – Van Helsing went to Exeter yesterday, and today he almost bounded into the room at about half past five o'clock, and thrust last night's *Westminster Gazette* into my hand.

"What do you think of that?" he asked, and pointed out a paragraph about children being decoyed away at Hampstead. It did not convey much to me, until I reached a passage where it described small punctured wounds on their throats.

"Well?" he said.

"It is like poor Lucy's."

"And what do you make of it?"

"Tell me!" I said. "I can hazard no opinion. I do not know what to think, and I have no data on which to found a conjecture."

"Do you mean to tell me, friend John, that you have no suspicion as to what poor Lucy died of; not after all the hints given, not only by events, but by me?"

"Of nervous prostration following on great loss or waste of blood."

"And how was the blood lost?" I shook my head. He stepped over and sat down beside me, and went on, "You are a clever man, friend John; you reason well, and your wit is bold; but you are too prejudiced. I want you to believe."

"To believe what?"

"You think that those so small holes in the children's throats were made by the same that made the hole in Miss Lucy?"

"I suppose so."

He stood up and said solemnly, "Then you are wrong. Oh, would it were so! But alas! No. It is worse, far, far worse."

"In God's name, Professor Van Helsing, what do you mean?"

He threw himself with a despairing gesture into a chair, and placed his elbows on the table, covering his face with his hands as he spoke: "They were made by Miss Lucy!"

For a while sheer anger mastered me; it was as if he had during her life struck Lucy on the face. I smote the table hard and rose up as I said to him, "Dr Van Helsing, are you mad?"

He raised his head and looked at me, and somehow the tenderness of his face calmed me at once.

"Would I were!" he said. "Madness were easy to bear compared with truth like this. Oh, my friend, even yet I do not expect you to believe. Tonight I go to prove it. Dare you come with me?"

This staggered me. A man does not like to prove such a truth.

He saw my hesitation, and took a key from his pocket and held it up.

"We spend the night, you and I, in the churchyard where Lucy lies. This is the key that lock the tomb."

My heart sank within me, for I felt that there was some fearful ordeal before us. I could do nothing, however, so I plucked up what heart I could and said that we had better hasten, as the afternoon was passing. Van Helsing said, "There is no hurry. Come, let us seek somewhere that we may eat, and then we shall go on our way."

We dined at "Jack Straw's Castle" along with a little crowd of bicyclists and others who were genially noisy. About ten o'clock we started from the inn.

It was then very dark, and the scattered lamps made the darkness greater when we were once outside their individual radius. The Professor had evidently noted the road we were

to go, for he went on unhesitatingly; but, as for me, I was in quite a mix-up as to locality.

At last we reached the wall of the churchyard, which we climbed over. With some little difficulty – for it was very dark, and the whole place seemed so strange to us – we found the Westenra tomb. The Professor took the key, opened the creaky door and, taking out a matchbox and a piece of candle, proceeded about his work systematically. Holding his candle so that he could read the coffin plates, he made assurance of Lucy's coffin. Another search in his bag, and he took out a turnscrew.

"What are you going to do?" I asked.

"To open the coffin. You shall yet be convinced."

Straight away he began taking out the screws, and finally lifted off the lid, showing the casing of lead beneath. Striking the turnscrew through the lead with a swift downward stab, which made me wince, he made a small hole.

I had expected a rush of gas from the week-old corpse, but the Professor never stopped for a moment; he sawed down a couple of feet along one side of the lead coffin, and then across, and down the other side. Taking the edge of the loose flange, he bent it back towards the foot of the coffin, and holding up the candle into the aperture, motioned to me to look.

I drew near and looked. The coffin was empty.

It was certainly a surprise to me, and gave me a considerable shock, but Van Helsing was unmoved. "Are you satisfied now, friend John?" he asked.

I felt all the dogged argumentativeness of my nature awake within me as I answered him, "I am satisfied that Lucy's body is not in that coffin; but that only proves one thing."

"And what is that, friend John?"

"That it is not there."

The Professor sighed. "Ah well!" he said. "We must have more proof. Come with me."

He put on the coffin lid again, gathered up all his things and placed them in the bag, blew out the light, and placed the candle also in the bag. We opened the door, and went out. Behind us he closed the door and locked it.

Then he told me to watch at one side of the churchyard whilst he would watch at the other. I took up my place behind a yew tree, and I saw his dark figure move until the intervening headstones and trees hid it from my sight.

It was a lonely vigil. Just after I had taken my place I heard a distant clock strike twelve, and in time came one and two. I was chilled and unnerved, and angry with the Professor for taking me on such an errand and with myself for coming. I was too cold and too sleepy to be keenly observant, and not sleepy enough to betray my trust; so altogether I had a dreary, miserable time.

Suddenly, as I turned round, I thought I saw something like a white streak, moving between two dark yew trees at the side of the churchyard farthest from the tomb; at the same time a dark mass moved from the Professor's side of the ground, and hurriedly went towards it.

Then I too moved; but I had to go round headstones and railed-off tombs, and I stumbled over graves. The sky was overcast, and somewhere far off an early cock crew.

A little way off, beyond a line of scattered juniper trees, a white, dim figure flitted in the direction of the tomb. I heard the rustle of actual movement where I had first seen the figure, and coming over, found the Professor holding in his arms a tiny child. When he saw me he held it out to me, and said, "Are you satisfied now?"

"No," I said, in a way that I felt was aggressive.

"Do you not see the child?"

"Yes, it is a child, but who brought it here? And is it wound-ed?" I asked.

"We shall see," said the Professor, and we took our way out of the churchyard, he carrying the sleeping child.

When we had got some little distance away, we went into a clump of trees, and struck a match, and looked at the child's throat. It was without a scratch or scar of any kind.

"Was I right?" I asked triumphantly.

"We were just in time," said the Professor thankfully.

We had now to decide what we were to do with the child, and so consulted about it. Finally we decided that we would take it to the Heath, and when we heard a policeman coming, would leave it where he could not fail to find it; we would then seek our way home as quickly as we could.

All fell out well. At the edge of Hampstead Heath we heard a policeman's heavy tramp, and laying the child on the path-way, we waited and watched until he saw it as he flashed his lantern to and fro. We heard his exclamation of astonish-ment, and then we went away silently. By good chance we got a cab near the "Spaniards", and drove to town.

I cannot sleep, so I make this entry. But I must try to get a few hours, as Van Helsing is to call for me at noon. He insists that I shall go with him on another expedition.

*　　*　　*

# THE EMPTY COFFIN

*27 September* – It was two o'clock before we found a suitable opportunity for our attempt. The funeral held at noon was all completed, and the last stragglers had taken themselves lazily away, when, looking carefully from behind a clump of alder trees, we saw the sexton lock the gate after him.

Again I felt that horrid sense of the reality of things, in which any effort of imagination seemed out of place; and I realized distinctly the perils of the law which we were incurring in our unhallowed work.

Besides, I felt it was all so useless. Outrageous as it was to open a leaden coffin, to see if a woman dead nearly a week were really dead, it now seemed the height of folly to open the tomb again, when we knew, from the evidence of our own eyesight, that the coffin was empty.

I shrugged my shoulders, however, and rested silent, for Van Helsing had a way of going on his own road, no matter who remonstrated. He took the key, opened the vault, and walked over to Lucy's coffin, and I followed.

He bent over and again forced back the leaden flange; and then a shock of surprise and dismay shot through me.

There lay Lucy, seemingly just as we had seen her the night before her funeral. She was, if possible, more radiantly beautiful than ever. The lips were red, nay redder than before; and on the cheeks was a delicate bloom.

"Are you convinced now?" said the Professor, and as he spoke he pulled back the lips and showed the teeth.

"See," he went on, "see, they are even sharper than before. With this and this" – and he touched one of the canine teeth and that below it – "the little children can be bitten. Are you of belief now, friend John?"

Once more, argumentative hostility woke within me. I *could* not accept such an overwhelming idea as he suggested; so, with an attempt to argue of which I was even at the moment ashamed, I said, "She may have been placed here since last night."

"By whom?"

"I do not know. Someone has done it."

"And yet she has been dead one week. Most peoples in that time would not look so."

I had no answer for this, so was silent. Van Helsing did not seem to notice. He was looking intently at the face, raising the eyelids and looking at the eyes, and once more opening the lips and examining the teeth. Then he turned to me and said, "She was bitten by the vampire when she was in a trance, sleep-walking. Oh, you start – you do not know that, friend John, but you shall know all later. In trance she died, and in trance she is Un-Dead, too. So it is that she differ from all other. Usually when the Un-Dead sleep at home" – he made a comprehensive sweep of his arm to designate what to a vampire was "home" – "their face show what they are. But this, so sweet, she go back to the nothings of the common dead. There is no malign there, see, and so it make hard that I must kill her in her sleep."

This turned my blood cold, and it began to dawn upon me that I was accepting Van Helsing's theories; if she were really dead, what was there of terror in the idea of killing her? He looked up at me, and evidently saw the change in my face, for he said almost joyously, "Ah, you believe now?"

I answered, "Do not press me too hard all at once. I am willing to accept. How will you do this bloody work?"

"I shall cut off her head and fill her mouth with garlic, and I shall drive a stake through her body."

It made me shudder to think of so mutilating the body of the woman whom I had loved. And yet the feeling was not so strong as I had expected. I was, in fact, beginning to shudder at the presence of this being, this Un-Dead, as Van Helsing called it, and to loathe it. Is it possible that love is all subjective, or all objective?

I waited a considerable time for Van Helsing to begin, but he stood as if wrapped in thought. Presently he closed his bag and said, "I have made up my mind. If you, who saw the wounds on Lucy's throat; if you, who saw the coffin empty last night and full today – if you know of this and yet of your own senses did not believe, how, then, can I expect Arthur to?

"He, poor fellow, must have one hour that will make the very face of heaven grow black to him; then we can act for good all round; and send him peace.

"My mind is made up. You return home to your asylum, and see that all be well. I shall spend the night here in this churchyard in my own way. Tomorrow night you will come to me to the Berkeley Hotel at ten of the clock.

"I shall send for Arthur to come too, and also that so fine young man of America that gave his blood. Later we shall all have work to do. I come with you so far as Piccadilly and there dine, for I must be back here before the sun set."

So we locked the tomb and came away, and got over the wall of the churchyard, which was not much of a task, and drove back to Piccadilly.

# 4

# The Bloodstained Mouth

Van Helsing needed Seward's belief, for without it he could hardly have gone on. But the next morning, the doctor's conviction – after a good night's sleep – was shaky once again. He wondered if Van Helsing was perhaps "unhinged", and tried to convince himself that there was a rational explanation to it all – if only he could find it.

Then he wondered – although with great reluctance – if the Professor might possibly have done the body-switching himself; if he was, in fact, quite mad – although still almighty clever. In the evening, when they all met up at the Berkeley Hotel as planned, instead of helping him in any way he merely stood and listened as Van Helsing set out his explanations and persuasions of the other two.

It was a hard task the Dutchman had: to tell Lord Godalming that his fiancée was not dead, but suspended in some weird and frightful limbo called "Un-Dead"; to tell him that he had a special dispensation to use the sacred wafer, called the "Host", to battle with the evil that possessed her; to tell him that they must go into her tomb, that they must open up her coffin.

Arthur, buffetted by wild emotions as he listened, first flared into anger, then groaned with anguish, then grew bone-white with despair. Van Helsing, in a kind of agony, concluded, "There are mysteries which men can only guess at, which age by age they may solve only in part. Believe me, we are now on the verge of one. But I have not done... May I cut off the head of dead Miss Lucy?"

Arthur cried out passionately his horrified refusal, and questioned Van Helsing's sanity. He had, said the Englishman, a duty to protect her grave from outrage – and by God, he would do it!

Van Helsing, who had been seated through all this, rose sternly then, and said he had a duty also, which he would also do "by God". All he wanted, he said, was for Lord Godalming to go with him, and to look and listen. After that, if need be, he would face the consequences – which meant, it seems, allow the young man to seek honour in a duel.

## Dr Seward's Diary

His voice broke a little, and he went on with a voice full of pity: "But, I beseech you, do not go forth in anger with me. In a long life of acts which were often not pleasant to do, and which sometimes did wring my heart, I have never had so heavy a task as now.

"Just think. For why should I give myself so much of labour and so much of sorrow? I have come here from my own land to do what I can of good; at the first to please my friend John, and then to help a sweet young lady, whom, too, I came to love. I gave to her my nights and days – before death, after death; and if my death can do her good even now, when she is the dead Un-Dead, she shall have it freely."

He said this with a very grave, sweet pride, and Arthur was much affected by it. He took the old man's hand and said in a broken voice, "Oh, it is hard to think of it, and I cannot understand; but at least I shall go with you and wait."

*Later* – It was just a quarter before twelve o'clock when we got into the churchyard over the low wall. The night was dark, with occasional gleams of moonlight between the rents of the heavy clouds that scudded across the sky. We all kept somehow close together, with Van Helsing slightly in front as he led the way.

When we had come close to the tomb I looked at Arthur, but he bore himself well. The Professor unlocked the door, and seeing a natural hesitation amongst us for various reasons, solved the difficulty by entering first himself.

The rest of us followed, and he closed the door. He then lit a dark lantern and pointed to the coffin. Arthur stepped forward hesitatingly; Van Helsing said to me, "You were with me here yesterday. Was the body of Miss Lucy in that coffin?"

"It was."

The Professor took his screwdriver and again took off the lid. Arthur looked on, very pale but silent. When he saw the rent in the lead, the blood rushed to his face for an instant, but as quickly fell away again, so that he remained of a ghastly whiteness. Van Helsing forced back the leaden flange, and we all looked in and recoiled.

The coffin was empty!

For several minutes no one spoke a word. The silence was broken by Quincey Morris. "Professor. Your word is all I want. Is this your doing?"

"I swear to you by all that I hold sacred that I have not removed nor touched her. What happened was this: Two nights ago my friend Seward and I came here, opened that coffin, and found it, as now, empty. We then waited, and saw something white come through the trees. The next day we came here in daytime, and she lay there. Did she not, friend John?"

"Yes."

"That night we were just in time. One more so small child was missing, and we find it, thank God, unharmed amongst the graves. Yesterday I came here before sundown, for at sundown the Un-Dead can move. I waited here all the night till the sun rose, but I saw nothing.

"But bear with me. So far there is much that is strange.

Wait you with me outside, unseen and unheard, and things much stranger are yet to be." He opened the door, and we filed out, he coming last and locking the door behind him.

Oh! But it seemed fresh and pure in the night air after the terror of that vault. How sweet it was to see the clouds race by, and the passing gleams of the moonlight, like the gladness and sorrow of a man's life. Each in his own way was solemn and overcome.

As to Van Helsing, he was employed in a definite way. First he took from his bag a mass of what looked like thin, wafer-like biscuit, which was carefully rolled up in a white napkin; next he took out a double handful of some whitish stuff, like dough or putty.

He crumbled the wafer up fine and worked it into the mass between his hands, then, rolling it into thin strips, began to lay them into the crevices between the door and its setting in the tomb. I was somewhat puzzled at this, and asked him what it was that he was doing.

"I am closing the tomb, so that the Un-Dead may not enter. It is the Host. I brought it from Amsterdam. I have an Indulgence."

It was an answer that appalled the most sceptical of us, and we felt individually that in the presence of such earnest purpose as the Professor's it was impossible to distrust. In respectful silence we took the places assigned to us close round the tomb, but hidden from the sight of anyone approaching.

There was a long spell of silence, a big, aching void, and then from the Professor a keen "S-s-s-s!" He pointed; and far down the avenue of yews we saw a white figure advance – a dim white figure, which held something dark at its breast.

The figure stopped, and at the moment a ray of moonlight fell between the masses of driving clouds and showed in startling prominence a dark-haired woman, dressed in the cerements of the grave.

We could not see the face, for it was bent down over what we saw to be a fair-haired child. There was a pause and a sharp little cry, such as a child gives in sleep, or a dog as it lies before the fire and dreams.

We were starting forward, but the Professor's warning hand, seen by us as he stood behind a yew tree, kept us back; and then as we looked the white figure moved forward again.

It was now near enough for us to see clearly, and the moonlight still held. My own heart grew cold as ice, and I could hear the gasp of Arthur, as we recognized the features of Lucy Westenra. Lucy Westenra, but yet how changed. The sweetness was turned to heartless cruelty, and the purity to voluptuous wantonness.

Van Helsing stepped out, and, obedient to his gesture, we all advanced too; the four of us ranged in a line before the door of the tomb. Van Helsing raised his lantern and drew the slide; by the concentrated light that fell on Lucy's face we could see that the lips were crimson with fresh blood, and that the stream had trickled over her chin and stained the purity of her lawn death-robe.

We shuddered with horror. I could see by the tremulous light that even Van Helsing's iron nerve had failed. Arthur was next to me, and if I had not seized his arm and held him up, he would have fallen.

When Lucy - I call the thing that was before us Lucy because it bore her shape - saw us, she drew back with an angry snarl, such as a cat gives when taken unawares; then her eyes ranged over us. Lucy's eyes in form and colour; but Lucy's eyes unclean and full of hellfire, instead of the pure, gentle orbs we knew.

At that moment the remnant of my love passed into hate and loathing; had she then to be killed, I could have done it with savage delight. As she looked, her eyes blazed with unholy light, and the face became wreathed with a voluptuous smile.

Oh, God, how it made me shudder to see it! With a careless motion, she flung to the ground the child that up to now she had clutched strenuously to her breast, growling over it as a dog growls over a bone. The child gave a sharp cry, and lay there moaning.

There was a cold-bloodedness in the act which wrung a groan from Arthur; when she advanced to him with outstretched arms and a wanton smile, he fell back and hid his face in his hands.

She still advanced, however, and with a languorous, voluptuous grace, said, "Come to me, Arthur. Leave these others and come to me. My arms are hungry for you. Come, and we can rest together. Come, my husband, come!"

Arthur seemed under a spell; moving his hands from his face, he opened wide his arms. She was leaping for them, when Van Helsing sprang forward and held between them his little golden crucifix. She recoiled from it, and, with a suddenly distorted face, full of rage, dashed past him as if to enter the tomb.

When within a foot or two of the door, however, she stopped as if arrested by some irresistible force. Then she turned, and her face was shown in the clear burst of moonlight and by the lamp.

Never did I see such baffled malice on a face; and never, I trust, shall such ever be seen again by mortal eyes. The beautiful colour became livid, the eyes seemed to throw out sparks

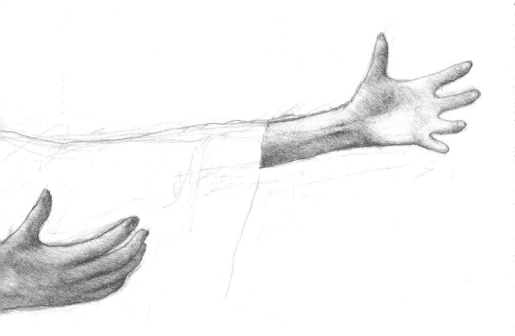

of hellfire, the lovely, bloodstained mouth grew to an open square. If ever a face meant death – if looks could kill – we saw it at that moment.

And so for full half a minute, which seemed an eternity, she remained between the lifted crucifix and the sacred closing of her means of entry. Van Helsing broke the silence by asking Arthur, "Answer me, oh my friend! Am I to proceed in my work?"

"Do as you will, friend; do as you will. There can be no horror like this ever any more!" And he groaned in spirit.

Quincey and I simultaneously moved towards him, and took his arms. We could hear the click of the closing lantern as Van Helsing held it down; coming close to the tomb, he began to remove from the chinks some of the sacred emblem which he had placed there.

We all looked on in horrified amazement as we saw, when he stood back, the woman, with a corporeal body as real at that moment as our own, pass in through the interstice where scarce a knife-blade could have gone. We all felt à glad sense of relief when we saw the Professor calmly restoring the strings of putty to the edges of the door.

When this was done, he lifted the child and said, "Come now, my friends; we can do no more till tomorrow. There is a funeral at noon, so here we shall all come before long after that. The friends of the dead will all be gone by two, and when the sexton lock the gate we shall remain.

"Then there is more to do; but not like this of tonight. As for this little one, he is not much harm, and by tomorrow night he shall be well. We shall leave him where the police will find him, as on the other night; and then to home."

Coming close to Arthur, he said, "My friend Arthur, you have had a sore trial; but after, when you will look back, you will see how it was necessary. You are now in the bitter waters, my child. By this time tomorrow you will, please God, have passed them, and have drunk of the sweet waters; so do not mourn overmuch. Till then I shall not ask you to forgive me."

Arthur and Quincey came home with me, and we tried to cheer each other on the way. We had left the child in safety, and were tired; so we all slept with more or less reality of sleep.

# 5

## Kiss Her Dead Lips

### Dr Seward's Diary

*29 September, night* – A little before twelve o'clock we three – Arthur, Quincey Morris and myself – called for the Professor. It was odd to notice that by common consent we had all put on black clothes.

We got to the churchyard by half-past one, and strolled about, keeping out of official observation, so that when the gravediggers had completed their task and the sexton had locked the gate, we had the place all to ourselves.

Van Helsing, instead of his little black bag, had with him a long leather one, something like a cricketing bag; it was manifestly of fair weight.

When we were alone and had heard the last of the footsteps die out up the road, we silently followed the Professor to the tomb. He unlocked the door, and we entered, closing it behind us.

Then he took from his bag the lantern, which he lit, and

also two wax candles, which, when lighted, he stuck, by melting their own ends, on other coffins, so that they might give light sufficient to work by.

When he again lifted the lid off Lucy's coffin we all looked - Arthur trembling like an aspen - and saw that the body lay there in all its death-beauty. But there was no love in my own heart, nothing but loathing for the foul Thing which had taken Lucy's shape without her soul.

I could see even Arthur's face grow hard as he looked. Presently he said to Van Helsing, "Is this really Lucy's body, or only a demon in her shape?"

"It is her body, and yet not it. But wait a while, and you shall see her as she was, and is."

She seemed like a nightmare of Lucy as she lay there; the pointed teeth, the bloodstained, voluptuous mouth, the whole carnal and unspiritual appearance, like a devilish mockery of sweet purity.

Van Helsing, with his usual methodicalness, began taking the various contents from his bag and placing them ready for use. First he took out a soldering iron and some plumbing solder, and then a small oil-lamp which burned at a fierce heat with a blue flame, then his operating knives. And last a round wooden stake, some two and a half or three inches thick and about three feet long.

One end of it was hardened by charring in the fire, and was sharpened to a fine point. With this stake came a heavy hammer, such as is used in the coal cellar for breaking lumps.

When all was ready, Van Helsing said, "Before we do any-thing, let me tell you this; it is out of the lore and experience of the ancients and of all those who have studied the powers of the Un-Dead.

"When they become such, there comes with the change the curse of immortality; they cannot die, but must go on age after age adding new victims and multiplying the evils of the world; for all that die from the preying of the Un-Dead become themselves Un-Dead, and prey on their kind.

"And so the circle goes on ever widening, like as the ripples from a stone thrown in the water.

"Friend Arthur, if you had met that kiss which you know of before poor Lucy die; or again, last night when you open your arms to her, you would in time, when you had died, have become *nosferatu*, as they call it in Eastern Europe, and would all time make more of those Un-Deads that so have filled us with horror.

"The career of this so unhappy dear lady is but just begun. Those children whose blood she suck are not as yet so much the worse; but if she live on, Un-Dead, more and more they lose their blood, and by her power over them they come to her; and so she draw their blood with that so wicked mouth.

"But if she die in truth, then all cease; the tiny wounds of the throats disappear, and they go back to their plays un-knowing ever of what has been.

"But of the most blessed of all, when this now Un-Dead be made to rest as true dead, then the soul of the poor lady whom we love shall again be free. Instead of working wickedness by night and growing more debased in the assimilation of it by day, she shall take her place with the other Angels.

"So that, my friend, it will be a blessed hand for her that shall strike the blow that sets her free. To this I am willing; but is there none amongst us who has a better right? Will it be no joy to think of hereafter, in the silence of the night when sleep is not: 'It was my hand that sent her to the stars, it was the hand of him that loved her best; the hand that of all she would herself have chosen, had it been to her to choose?' Tell me if there be such a one amongst us?"

We all looked at Arthur. He stepped forward and said bravely, though his hand trembled, and his face was as pale as

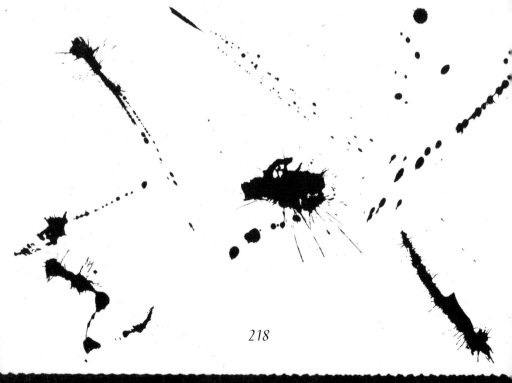

snow, "My true friend, from the bottom of my broken heart, I thank you. I shall not falter!"

Van Helsing laid a hand on his shoulder, and said, "Brave lad! A moment's courage, and it is done. It will be a fearful ordeal, but it will be only a short time, and you will then rejoice more than your pain was great; from this grim tomb you will emerge as though you tread on air."

"Go on," said Arthur hoarsely. "Tell me what I am to do."

"Take this stake in your left hand, ready to place the point over the heart, and the hammer in your right. Then when we begin our prayer for the dead – I shall read him and the others shall follow – strike in God's name, that so all may be well with the dead that we love, and that the Un-Dead pass away."

Arthur took the stake and the hammer, and when once his mind was set on action his hands never trembled nor even quivered. Van Helsing began to read, and Quincey and I followed as well as we could. Arthur placed the point over the heart, and as I looked I could see its dint in the white flesh. Then he struck with all his might.

The Thing in the coffin writhed; and a hideous, blood-curdling screech came from the opened red lips. The body shook and quivered and twisted in wild contortions; the sharp white teeth champed together till the lips were cut, and the mouth was smeared with a crimson foam.

But Arthur never faltered. He looked like a figure of Thor as his untrembling arm rose and fell, driving deeper and deeper the mercy-bearing stake, whilst the blood from the pierced heart welled and spurted up around it. His face was set, and high duty seemed to shine through it; the sight of it gave us courage, so that our voices seemed to ring through the little vault.

And then the writhing and quivering of the body became less, and the teeth ceased to champ, and the face to quiver. Finally it lay still. The terrible task was over.

The hammer fell from Arthur's hand. He reeled and would have fallen had we not caught him. The great drops of sweat sprang out on his forehead, and his breath came in broken gasps. For a few minutes we were so taken up with him that we did not look towards the coffin.

When we did, however, a murmur of startled surprise ran from one to the other of us. We gazed so eagerly that Arthur rose, for he had been seated on the ground, and came and looked too; and then a glad, strange light broke over his face and dispelled altogether the gloom of horror that lay upon it.

There in the coffin lay no longer the foul Thing that we had so dreaded, but Lucy as we had seen her in her life, with her face of unequalled sweetness and purity. One and all we felt the holy calm that lay like sunshine over the wasted face and form.

Van Helsing came and laid his hand on Arthur's shoulder, and said to him, "And now, Arthur, my friend, dear lad, am I not forgiven?"

The reaction of the terrible strain came as he took the old man's hand in his, and raising it to his lips, pressed it, and said, "Forgiven! God bless you that you have given my dear one her soul again, and me peace." He put his hands on the Professor's shoulder, and laying his head on his breast, cried for a while silently, whilst we stood unmoving.

When he raised his head Van Helsing said to him, "And now, my child, you may kiss her. Kiss her dead lips if you will, as she would have you to, if for her to choose. For she is not a grinning devil now – not any more a foul Thing for all eternity. No longer she is the devil's Un-Dead. She is God's true dead, whose soul is with Him!"

Arthur bent and kissed her, and then we sent him and Quincey out of the tomb; the Professor and I sawed the top off the stake, leaving the point of it in the body.

Then we cut off the head and filled the mouth with garlic. We soldered up the leaden coffin, screwed on the lid, and gathering up our belongings, came away. When the Professor locked the door he gave the key to Arthur.

Outside the air was sweet, the sun shone, and the birds sang, and it seemed as if all nature were tuned to a different pitch. There was gladness and mirth and peace everywhere, for we were at rest ourselves on one account, and we were glad, though it was with a tempered joy.

Before we moved away Van Helsing said, "Now, my friends, one step of our work is done, one the most harrowing to ourselves. But there remains a greater task: to find out the author of all this our sorrow and to stamp him out.

"I have clues which we can follow; but it is a long task, and a difficult one, and there is danger in it, and pain. Shall you not all help me? We have learned to believe, all of us – is it not so? And since so, do we not see our duty? Yes! And do we not promise to go on to the bitter end?"

Each in turn, we took his hand, and the promise was made. Then said the Professor as we moved off, "Two nights hence you shall meet with me and dine together at seven of the clock with friend John. I shall entreat two others, two that you know not as yet; and I shall be ready to all our work and our plans unfold.

"Friend John, you come with me home, for I have much to consult about, and you can help me. Tonight I leave for Amsterdam, but shall return tomorrow night.

"And then begins our great quest. Then our promise shall be made to each other anew; for there is a terrible task before us, and once our feet are on the ploughshare, we must not draw back."

Book Four
THE PASSION
of MINA HARKER

# 1

# The Lunatic Asylum

*The centre chosen for their operations against the evil of Count Dracula was, appropriately, an insane asylum. Mina Harker was the first to be installed there, having come up from Exeter without Jonathan, who had gone to Whitby seeking information.*

*She was met at Paddington Station by Dr Seward, who had been given a copy of her diary and Jonathan's by Van Helsing but had not had time, as yet, to read them.*

*After some time waiting at the station, as he put it in his journal:* I was beginning to feel uneasy, lest I might miss my guest, when a sweet-faced, dainty-looking girl stepped up to me, and, after a quick glance, said: "Dr Seward, is it not?"

"And you are Mrs Harker!" I answered at once; whereupon she held out her hand.

"I knew you from the description of poor dear Lucy; but—" She stopped suddenly; a quick blush overspread her face.

The blush that rose to my own cheeks somehow set us both at ease, for it was a tacit answer to her own. I got her luggage, which included a typewriter, and we took the Underground to Fenchurch Street, after I had sent a wire to my housekeeper to have a sitting-room and bedroom prepared at once.

In due time we arrived. She knew, of course, that the place was a lunatic asylum, but I could see that she was unable to repress a slight shudder when we entered.

*The two of them hit it off, however, and were soon at their ease. Mina was given Seward's phonograph cylinders to listen to while he caught up on her typescripts. The terrible details each had to absorb about the other's life – and those of their mutual friends – led to great sympathy. By the time Jonathan arrived, they had a bond of trust and understanding.*

*In Whitby, Jonathan's main task had been to track down the boxes brought ashore from the* Demeter – *and the discovery that they had been delivered to the house next door to his asylum struck Seward like a hammer blow.*

*"Goodness knows," he recorded, "we had enough clues from the conduct of the patient Renfield! Oh, if we had only had them earlier we might have saved poor Lucy!"*

*The other fact implicit in such clues – that somehow Dracula had targeted both people and locations with foresight from afar – remained quite overlooked. In terms of subtle power, the Count was far ahead of anything the Professor had yet guessed.*

*Jonathan, though – in charge of collating all material – was edging near the truth. Firstly, he began to realize that Renfield might somehow be the key.*

## Dr Seward's Diary

*30 September* – Harker thinks that I should see Renfield, as hitherto he has been a sort of index to the coming and going of the Count. I hardly see this yet, but when I get at the dates I suppose I shall.

I found Renfield sitting placidly in his room with his hands folded, smiling benignly. At the moment he seemed as sane as anyone I ever saw.

He spoke of going home, a subject he has never mentioned to my knowledge during his sojourn here. In fact, he spoke quite confidently of getting his discharge at once.

I believe that, had I not had the chat with Harker and read the letters and the dates of his outbursts, I should have been prepared to sign for him after a brief time of observation. As it is, I am darkly suspicious.

All those outbreaks were in some way linked with the proximity of the Count. He is himself zoophagous, and in his wild ravings outside the chapel door of the deserted house he always spoke of "master".

So I came away. I mistrust these quiet moods of his; so I have given the attendant a hint to look closely after him, and to have a strait-waistcoat ready in case of need.

⋆   ⋆   ⋆

*On the same day, both Godalming and Quincey Morris arrived, and were equally bowled over by Mrs Harker's competence and beauty.*

*Arthur, indeed, soon found himself sobbing in her arms over the loss of Lucy, while Quincey, as he had with Lucy Westenra, sufficiently bewitched her to receive a kiss – and called her, calmly, "little girl".*

*Mina wrote: "Little girl! – the very words he had used to Lucy, and oh, but he proved himself a friend!"*

*Later, with all serene once more, she asked Dr Seward if she might see Renfield, too. "She looked so appealing and so pretty," he wrote (hardly scientifically!), "that I could not refuse her." The meeting was to prove a little bizarre – but first the maniac insisted on making his room fit for such a visitor.*

### *Dr Seward's Diary*

His method of tidying was peculiar: he simply swallowed all the flies and spiders in the boxes before I could stop him. When he had got through his disgusting task, he said cheerfully, "Let the lady come in," and sat down on the edge of his bed with his head down, but with his eyelids raised so that he could see her as she entered.

"Good evening, Mr Renfield," said she. "Dr Seward has told me of you."

He made no immediate reply, but eyed her all over intently with a set frown on his face; then to my intense astonishment he said, "You're not the girl the doctor wanted to marry, are you? You can't be, you know, for she's dead."

"Oh no! I have a husband of my own, to whom I was married before I ever saw Dr Seward, or he me. I am Mrs Harker."

"Then what are you doing here?"

"My husband and I are staying on a visit."

"Then don't stay."

"But why not?"

At this point, Seward, thinking that "this style of conversation might not be pleasant to Mrs Harker", tried to steer it to calmer waters, which made the madman – who clearly wished to tell her something that he thought important, but which he could not say directly – treat him, rudely, like a fool. Seward called the meeting to an end.

Whatever Mina's feelings on the matter, she remained polite, and friendly.

"Goodbye," she told Renfield, "and I hope I may see you often, under auspices pleasanter to yourself."

Without a hint of bitterness, he issued what turned out to be a chilling warning as he replied, "Goodbye, my dear. I pray God I may never see your sweet face again. May He bless and keep you!"

# 2

# A Solemn Compact

*Van Helsing was the last to reach the madhouse, and soon took up the reins of leadership. He was, as usual, fulsome in his praise of "Madam Mina", but, with a lack of imagination worthy of his pupil Seward, decided that her best use to them was as a simple secretary.*

*Mina – a good, loyal late-Victorian young lady and obedient new wife – swallowed this without a protest, even when its full implications later emerged. Like so many of the men's decisions, it was to prove disastrous.*

### Mina Harker's Journal

*30 September* – When we met in Dr Seward's study two hours after dinner, Professor Van Helsing made me sit next to him on his right, and asked me to act as secretary; Jonathan sat next to me. Opposite us were Lord Godalming, Dr Seward and Mr Morris.

The Professor said, "It were, I think, good that I tell you

something of the kind of enemy with which we have to deal. We then can discuss how we shall act, and can take our measure according.

"There are such beings as vampires. Even had we not the proof of our own unhappy experience, the teachings and the records of the past give proof enough. This vampire which is amongst us is of himself so strong in person as twenty men; he is of cunning more than mortal. He can direct the elements: the storm, the fog, the thunder; he can command all the meaner things: the rat, and the owl, and the bat - the moth, and the fox, and the wolf; he can grow and become small; and he can at times vanish and come unknown.

"How then are we to begin our strife to destroy him? How shall we find his where; and having found it, how can we destroy? My friends, it is a terrible task, for if we fail he must surely win; and then where end we? To fail is not mere life or death. It is that we become as him; that we become foul things of the night - without heart or conscience, preying on the bodies and the souls of those we love best.

"To us for ever are the gates of heaven shut; for who shall open them to us again? We go on for all time abhorred by all; a blot on the face of God's sunshine; an arrow in the side of Him who died for man. But we are face to face with duty; and in such case must we shrink? What say you?"

Whilst he was speaking Jonathan had taken my hand; it was life to me to feel its touch. When the Professor had done, my husband looked in my eyes, and I in his; there was no need for speaking between us.

"I answer for Mina and myself," he said.

"Count me in, Professor," said Mr Quincey Morris, laconically as usual.

"I am with you," said Lord Godalming, "for Lucy's sake, if for no other reason."

Dr Seward simply nodded.

The Professor stood up and, after laying his golden crucifix on the table, held out his hand on either side. I took his right hand, and Lord Godalming his left; Jonathan held my right with his left and stretched across to Mr Morris.

So as we all took hands our solemn compact was made. I felt my heart icy cold, but it did not even occur to me to draw back. We resumed our places, and Dr Van Helsing went on with a sort of cheerfulness which showed that the serious work had begun. It was to be taken as gravely, and in as businesslike a way, as any other transaction of life.

"Well, you know what we have to contend against; but we, too, are not without strength. We have on our side resources of science; we are free to act and think; and the hours of the day and the night are ours equally. We have self-devotion in a cause, and an end to achieve which is not a selfish one. These things are much.

"Now let us see how far the general powers arrayed against us are restrict. In fine, let us consider the limitations of the vampire in general, and of this one in particular.

"All we have to go upon are traditions and superstitions. For, let me tell you, he is known everywhere that men have been. In old Greece, in old Rome, in Germany, in France, in India, in China. The vampire live on, and cannot die by mere passing of the time; he can flourish when that he can fatten on the blood of the living. Even more, he can grow younger.

"He throws no shadow, he make in the mirror no reflect, he has the strength of many, he can transform himself, he can come in mist, he come on moonlight rays as elemental dust – Ah, but hear me through.

"He can do all these things, yet he is not free. Nay, he is even more prisoner than the slave of the galley, than the madman in his cell. He may not enter anywhere, unless there be someone of the household who bid him to; his power ceases at the coming of the day. If he be not at the place whither he is bound, he can only change himself at noon or at exact sunrise or sunset. It is said, too, that he can only pass running water at the slack or the flood of the tide.

"Then there are things which so afflict him that he has no power, as the garlic that we know of; and things sacred, as this symbol, my crucifix. The branch of wild rose on his coffin keep him that he move not from it; a sacred bullet fired into the coffin kill him so that he be true dead; and as for the stake through him, we know already of its peace; or the cut-off head that giveth rest. We have seen it with our eyes."

Mr Morris now got up quietly, and went out of the room. There was a little pause, and then the Professor went on.

"And now we must settle what we do. We have here much data, and we must proceed to lay out our campaign. We know from the enquiry of Jonathan that from the castle to Whitby came fifty boxes of earth, all of which were delivered at Carfax; we also know that at least some of these boxes have been removed.

"It seems to me, that our first step should be to ascertain whether all the rest remain in the house beyond that wall where we look today; or whether any more have been removed. If the latter, we must trace—"

Here we were interrupted in a very startling way. Outside the house came the sound of a pistol-shot; the glass of the window was shattered with a bullet, which struck the far wall of the room. We heard Mr Morris's voice without: "Sorry! I fear I have alarmed you. I shall come in and tell you about it."

A minute later he came in and said, "It was an idiotic thing of me to do, and I ask your pardon, Mrs Harker, most sincerely. But the fact is that whilst the Professor was talking there came a big bat and sat on the windowsill. I have got such a horror of the damned brutes from recent events that I went out to have a shot."

"Did you hit it?" asked Dr Van Helsing.

"I don't know; I fancy not, for it flew away into the wood."

Without saying any more he took his seat, and the Professor began to resume his statement.

"We must trace each of these boxes; and when we are ready, we must either capture or kill this monster in his lair; or we must, so to speak, sterilize the earth, so that no more he can seek safety in it. Thus in the end we may find him in his form of man between the hours of noon and sunset, and so engage with him when he is at his most weak."

*At this point, the Dutchman dropped a bombshell – one he had already agreed, it emerged, with Dr Seward. They clearly thought they were doing Mina a favour.*

*"And now for you, Madam Mina," Van Helsing said, "this night is the end until all be well. You are too precious to us to have such risk.*

*"When we part tonight, you no more must question. We shall tell you all in good time. We are men, and are able to bear; but you must be our star and our hope, and we shall act all the more free that you are not in the danger, such as we are."*

## Mina Harker's Journal

All the men, even Jonathan, seemed relieved; but it did not seem to me good that they should brave danger and, perhaps, lessen their safety – strength being the best safety – through care of me; but their minds were made up, and, though it was a bitter pill to swallow, I could say nothing, save to accept.

MINA HARKER'S JOURNAL

*Despite the fact the meeting had lasted until the early hours, Quincey Morris, ever eager, proposed that they go immediately next door to Carfax to see what they could do to thwart the vampire – and Mina bit her lip on any comment she might have wished to make. Shortly afterwards her husband and their friends had left her in the lunatic asylum.*

*Mina Harker's Journal*

Manlike, they have told me to go to bed and sleep; as if a woman can sleep when those she loves are in danger! I shall lie down and pretend to sleep, lest Jonathan have added anxiety about me when he returns.

*Manlike too, perhaps, to have abandoned her at such a time, in such a place. One of the inmates, it was soon to be revealed, would not have done such a dangerous and stupid thing.*

# 3

# Rats and Corruption

*That inmate, Renfield, in fact sent a message to Dr Seward in greatest haste just before the men were about to leave. It was four o'clock in the morning, but he wished to raise a matter of the "utmost importance", which could not wait. Seward went reluctantly and, at their own request, took Van Helsing and the others with him.*

*Renfield, although in a state of excitement, was rational in the extreme. He shook hands with his new visitors, talked intelligently and calmly, and argued that he was now completely sane – and he wanted his release. Even Seward, despite himself, was most impressed.*

*He was not, however, quite convinced, and suggested not unreasonably that they could talk more in the morning. Renfield was not satisfied.*

*"I fear," he told the doctor, "that you hardly apprehend my wish. I desire to go at once – here – now – this very hour – this very moment, if I may."*

When turned down once again, he began to plead – still calm, still rational. It was not for his sake, he said, but for the sake of others – his reasons "springing from the highest sense of duty". But he would not give those reasons; he said he could not.

Even when Van Helsing stepped in Renfield could not be swayed. The Professor said that if Renfield could satisfy him, Van Helsing, with his actual reason "for wishing to be free tonight", he would secure that freedom from Dr Seward. Renfield replied that he could not, saying, "I am not my own master in the matter," at which Jack Seward lost his patience.

He said briskly: "Come, my friends, we have work to do. Goodnight." And Renfield began to slide towards the frantic.

*Dr Seward's Diary*

He threw himself on his knees, and held up his hands, wringing them in plaintive supplication, and poured forth a torrent of entreaty, with the tears rolling down his cheeks and his whole face and form expressive of the deepest emotion.

"Let me entreat you, Dr Seward, oh, let me implore you, to let me out of this house at once. Send me away how you will and where you will; send keepers with me with whips and chains; let them take me in a strait-waistcoat, manacled and leg-ironed, even to a gaol; but let me go out of this.

"You don't know what you do by keeping me here. I am speaking from the depths of my heart – of my very soul. You don't know whom you wrong, or how; and I may not tell. Woe is me! I may not tell. By all you hold sacred – by all you hold dear – by your love that is lost – by your hope that lives – for the sake of the Almighty, take me out of this and save my soul from guilt!

"Can't you hear me, man? Can't you understand? Will you never learn? Don't you know that I am sane and earnest now; that I am no lunatic in a mad fit, but a sane man fighting for his soul? Oh, hear me! Hear me! Let me go! Let me go! Let me go!"

I thought that the longer this went on the wilder he would get, and so would bring on a fit; so I took him by the hand and raised him up.

"Come," I said sternly, "no more of this; we have had quite

enough already. Get to your bed and try to behave more discreetly."

He suddenly stopped and looked at me intently for several moments. Then, without a word, he rose and, moving over, sat down on the side of the bed.

When I was leaving the room, he said to me in a quiet, well-bred voice, "You will, I trust, Dr Seward, do me the justice to bear in mind, later on, that I did what I could to convince you tonight."

*In truth, they could not have had a starker warning, albeit from a lunatic. The men ignored it, and went off to hunt for more important clues...*

*The story of the Carfax search was taken up by Jonathan Harker. Van Helsing, he recorded, issued to each of them a silver crucifix, a neck-wreath of garlic flowers, a knife – for Jonathan a great, curved Kukri – a revolver, an electric torch and an envelope containing a small piece of the Host. Lord Godalming, strangely, went and got a silver whistle.*

*Then, with skeleton keys, John Seward made an entrance to the house and each man lit his torch. The whole place, Jonathan wrote, was thick with dust and cobwebs, but he could lead them to the chapel as he had been inside the house before, when surveying it before the sale. Very soon the chapel door was creaking open...*

## Jonathan Harker's Journal

*1 October, 5 a.m.* – We were prepared for some unpleasantness, for as we were opening the door a faint, malodorous air seemed to exhale through the gaps, but none of us ever expected such an odour as we encountered.

None of the others had met the Count at all at close quarters, and when I had seen him he was either in the fasting stage of his existence in his rooms or in a ruined building open to the air; but here the place was small and close, and the long disuse had made the air stagnant and foul.

How shall I describe it? It was not alone that it was composed of all the ills of mortality and with the pungent, acrid smell of blood, but it seemed as though corruption had become itself corrupt. Faugh! It sickens me to think of it. Every breath exhaled by that monster seemed to have clung to the place and intensified its loathsomeness.

Under ordinary circumstances such a stench would have brought our enterprise to an end; but this was no ordinary case, and the high and terrible purpose in which we were involved gave us a strength which rose above merely physical considerations. A glance was sufficient to show the great earth chests. There were twenty-nine left out of fifty.

Suddenly, for an instant, my heart stood still. Somewhere, looking out from the shadow, I seemed to see the highlights of the Count's evil face, the ridge of the nose, the red eyes, the red lips, the awful pallor. It was only for a moment, and

I turned my lamp in the direction, and there was no sign of anyone. I took it that fear had helped imagination, and said nothing.

A few minutes later I saw Morris step suddenly back from a corner, which he was examining. We all followed his movements with our eyes, for undoubtedly some nervousness was growing on us, and we saw a whole mass of phosphorescence, which twinkled like stars. The whole place was becoming alive with rats.

For a moment or two we stood appalled, all save Lord Godalming, who was seemingly prepared for such an emergency. Rushing over to the great iron-bound oaken door, he turned the key in the lock, drew the huge bolts, and swung the door open. Then, taking his little silver whistle from his pocket, he blew a low, shrill call.

It was answered from behind Dr Seward's house by the yelping of dogs, and after about a minute three terriers came dashing round the corner.

Even in the minute that had elapsed, the number of rats had vastly increased, till the lamplight, shining on their moving dark bodies and glittering, baleful eyes, made the place look like a bank of earth set with fireflies. The dogs dashed on, but at the threshold suddenly stopped and snarled, and then, simultaneously lifting their noses, began to howl in most lugubrious fashion. The rats were multiplying in thousands, and we moved out.

Lord Godalming lifted one of the dogs and, carrying him in, placed him on the floor. The instant his feet touched the ground he seemed to recover his courage, and rushed at his natural enemies. They fled before him so fast that before he had shaken the life out of a score, the other dogs, who had by now been lifted in in the same manner, had but small prey ere the whole mass had vanished.

We closed the outer door and barred and locked it, and bringing the dogs with us, began our search of the house. We found nothing throughout except dust in extraordinary proportions, and all untouched save for my own footsteps when I had made my first visit. Never once did the dogs exhibit any symptom of uneasiness, and even when we returned to the chapel they frisked about as though they had been rabbit-hunting in a summer wood.

The morning was quickening in the east when we emerged from the front. Dr Van Helsing locked the door, putting the key into his pocket.

"So far," he said, "our night has been eminently successful. No harm has come to us such as I feared might be, and yet we have ascertained how many boxes are missing. More than all do I rejoice that our first step has been accomplished without the bringing thereinto our most sweet Madam Mina. We have reason to be content with our first night's work."

The house was silent when we got back, save for some poor creature who was screaming away in one of the distant wards, and a low, moaning sound from Renfield's room. The poor wretch was doubtless torturing himself, after the manner of the insane, with needless thoughts of pain.

I came tiptoe into our own room, and found Mina asleep, breathing so softly that I had to put my ear down to hear it. She looks paler than usual. I rest on the sofa, so as not to disturb her.

*Later* – I suppose it was natural that we should have all over-slept ourselves, for the night had no rest at all. Even Mina must have felt its exhaustion, for though I slept till the sun was high, I was awake before her, and had to call two or three times before she awoke.

Indeed, she was so sound asleep that for a few seconds she did not recognize me, but looked at me with a sort of blank terror, as one looks who has been waked out of a bad dream. She complained a little of being tired, and I let her rest till later in the day.

We now know of twenty-one boxes having been removed, and we may be able to trace them all. Such will, of course, immensely simplify our labour, and the sooner the matter is attended to the better.

*Jonathan, indeed, began the task of tracing them later that very day – 1 October – by going off to London. The other men worked at related matters, with Van Helsing thinking and studying* demonically. When Mina reawoke, though, she found herself in a disturbing state – low-spirited, anxious and "strangely sad".

From her journal entry of later in the day, although she did not realize it herself, it was obvious that something dreadful had happened to her while the men were in the chapel next door.

In retrospect, also, Renfield's desperate attempts to secure his release before the men went into Carfax are explained.

He had been trying to warn them that it was his duty, fate, destiny – which he could not reveal in words – to "invite" Count Dracula into the asylum when they had gone ... for without an invitation on a first occasion, a vampire cannot enter anywhere.

When release was ruled out, his frantic desperation to be removed from the building – guarded with whips and chains, in leg-irons, anything – is similarly explained. "Take me out of this," he said, "and save my soul from guilt!" In the asylum, left alone, he knew that he was bound to betray this poor, sweet girl.

Mina knew nothing, except that she felt low, and could not stop herself from crying now and then...

4

# Mina's Dreams

*That afternoon Mina wrote up her night memories in her journal. She had gone to bed at roughly 4 a.m.*

## Mina Harker's Journal

1 October – I can't quite remember how I fell asleep. I remember hearing the sudden barking of the dogs and a lot of queer sounds, like praying on a very tumultuous scale, from Mr Renfield's room, which is somewhere under this. And then there was silence over everything, silence so profound that it startled me, and I got up and looked out of the window.

All was dark and silent, the black shadows thrown by the moonlight seeming full of a mystery of their own. Not a thing seemed to be stirring, but all to be grim and fixed as death or fate; so that a thin streak of white mist, that crept with almost imperceptible slowness across the grass towards the house, seemed to have a sentience and a vitality of its own.

The poor man was more loud than ever, and though I could not distinguish a word he said, I could in some way recognize some passionate entreaty. Then there was the sound of a struggle, and I knew that the attendants were dealing with him. I was so frightened that I crept into bed, and pulled the clothes over my head, putting my fingers in my ears.

I thought that I was asleep, and waiting for Jonathan to come back; then it began to dawn upon me that the air was heavy, and dank, and cold. I put back the clothes from my face, and found, to my surprise, that all was dim around me. The gaslight which I had left lit for Jonathan, but turned down, came only like a tiny red spark through the fog, which had evidently grown thicker and poured into the room.

Then it occurred to me that I had shut the window before I had come to bed. I would have got out to make certain on the point, but some leaden lethargy seemed to chain my limbs and even my will. I lay still and endured; that was all.

The mist grew thicker and thicker, till it seemed a sort of pillar of cloud through the top of which I could see the light of the gas shining like a red eye. Suddenly the horror burst upon me that it was thus that Jonathan had seen those awful women growing into reality through the whirling mist in the moonlight, and in my dream I must have fainted, for all became black darkness.

The last conscious effort which imagination made was to show me a livid white face bending over me out of the mist. I must be careful of such dreams, for they would unseat one's reason if there were too much of them. I would get Dr Van Helsing or Dr Seward to prescribe something for me which would make me sleep, only that I fear to alarm them.

Tonight I shall strive hard to sleep naturally. If I do not, I shall tomorrow night get them to give me a dose of chloral. Last night tired me more than if I had not slept at all.

*As well as writing in her journal, Mina, while Jonathan was in London, spent the hours reading and dozing fitfully. At some time Renfield asked if he might see her in his cell, and was "very gentle", she recorded.*

*"When I came away," wrote Mina, "he kissed my hand and bade God bless me. Some way it affected me much; I am crying when I think of him. This is a new weakness. Jonathan would be miserable if he knew."*

*Jonathan did not know, however, for he returned from London after Mina had gone to sleep. Next morning – when she woke feeling "weak and spiritless" – he caught the train again for another full day's tracking, and none of the men returned till* dinner time. After the meal they sent Mina off to bed, because "they wanted to tell each other what had occurred to each during the day; I could see from Jonathan's manner that he had something important to communicate."

Now fully excluded from the powerhouse of male thinking – a mistake that led to more disaster very soon – Mina, dutiful as ever, accepted her dismissal. But she did ask Dr Seward for a sleeping draught, which he assured her was very mild. It was not until she was dropping off, unfortunately, that she felt a small nag of doubt. She recorded:

2 October, 10 p.m. – I hope I have not done wrong, for as sleep begins to flirt with me, a new fear comes: that I may have been foolish in thus depriving myself of the power of waking. I might want it. Here comes sleep. Goodnight.

Mina's fear, her nagging premonition, was sadly well-founded. For in the two days that the men had blindly gone about their investigations and neglected her, Dracula had been building up towards an act of total domination. What's more, they were on a wave of self-congratulation: they thought that they were getting close to victory.

On 1 October, the morning after Mina's first "dream", Jonathan had traced the hauliers who had shifted the boxes of earth from the chapel, and had pinpointed twelve of them to an address in Bethnal Green, east London.

By the next day his searching had struck gold. The nine

remaining boxes had been accounted for – as having gone to an empty house in Piccadilly. Jonathan had located the property, noted it had recently been sold, and sought further information from the estate agents who had handled it.

The buyer, undoubtedly, had been Dracula.

Both evenings after his exertions Jonathan returned to the asylum at Purfleet to inform the others of his progress – but they themselves had not been wasting time. Arthur and Quincey Morris had been checking out horses, in case of need when the hunt got hot. The plan was to locate all the boxes between sunrise and sunset, and leave the vampire without a refuge by "sterilizing" the foul earth.

Van Helsing, meanwhile, had been in the British Museum "searching for witch and demon cures." Seward commented laconically: "I sometimes think we must be all mad and that we shall wake to sanity in strait-waistcoats."

After both long days Jonathan had found his wife listless, pale, exhausted – and his heart went out to her. In fact, after he had looked at her asleep – and drugged – in bed on the second night, 2 October, he recorded in his journal, "Thank God, this will be the last night of her feeling the sting of our not showing our confidence. I am glad we made our resolution in time, as our growing knowledge would be torture to her."

His loyal wife, Jonathan decided, must go back to Exeter alone, the very next morning, for her own good. Then, satisfied and dog-tired, he rolled into bed beside her and went straight to sleep.

The other men had
all retired too, although
Dr Seward, at least, was
still awake. He was noting in
his diary, with some satisfaction,
that the next day might see "the
beginning of the end; the destruction
of the monster."

At which point he heard a yell, and an
attendant came bursting into his room.
Renfield, he reported, had had an accident – and was lying face
downward on his floor, covered in blood.

The complacency was about to be shattered. For good.

# 5

## The Glittering Pool of Blood

*Seward, when he got the news, naturally abandoned his diary entry. It was the following day before he took up his pen again.*

### Dr Seward's Diary

*3 October* – When I came to Renfield's room I found him lying on the floor on his left side in a glittering pool of blood. When I went to move him, it became at once apparent that he had received some terrible injuries.

As the face was exposed I could see that it was horribly bruised, as though it had been beaten against the floor – indeed it was from the face wounds that the pool of blood originated. The attendant who was kneeling beside the body said to me as we turned him over, "I think, sir, his back is broken. See, both his right arm and leg and the whole side of his face are paralysed."

How such a thing could have happened puzzled the attendant beyond measure. He seemed quite bewildered. I said to him, "Go to Dr Van Helsing, and ask him to kindly come here at once. I want him without an instant's delay." The man ran off, and within a very few minutes the Professor appeared.

Almost before he looked at the patient, he whispered to me, "Send the attendant away. We must be alone with him when he becomes conscious."

The man withdrew, and we went into a strict examination. The wounds of the face were superficial; the real injury was a depressed fracture of the skull, extending right up through the motor area. The Professor thought a moment and said, "We must reduce the pressure and get back to normal conditions, as far as can be; we must trephine at once or it may be too late."

As he was speaking there was a soft tapping at the door. I went and opened it and found in the corridor Arthur and Quincey in pyjamas and slippers. The former spoke: "I heard your man call up Dr Van Helsing and tell him of an accident. May we come in?"

Quincey said softly, "My God! What has happened to him? Poor, poor devil!" I told him briefly, and added that we expected he would recover consciousness after the operation – for a short time at all events.

"We shall wait," said Van Helsing, "just long enough to fix the best spot for trephining, so that we may most quickly and perfectly remove the blood clot; for it is evident that the haemorrhage is increasing."

The minutes during which we waited passed with fearful slowness. I had a horrible sinking in my heart, and from Van Helsing's face I gathered that he felt some fear or apprehension as to what was to come.

The poor man's breathing came in uncertain gasps. Each instant he seemed as though he would open his eyes and speak; but then would follow a prolonged stertorous breath, and he would relapse into a more fixed insensibility. Inured as I was to sickbeds and death, this suspense grew and grew upon me. I could almost hear the beating of my own heart; and the blood surging through my temples sounded like blows from a hammer.

At last there came a time when it was evident that the patient was sinking fast; he might die at any moment. I looked up at the Professor and caught his eyes fixed on mine. Without another word he made the operation.

For a few moments the breathing continued to be stertorous. Then there came a breath so prolonged that it seemed as though it would tear open his chest. Suddenly his eyes opened, and became fixed in a wild, helpless stare. He moved convulsively, and as he did so, said, "I'll be quiet, Doctor. Tell them to take off the strait-waistcoat. I have had a terrible dream, and it has left me so weak that I cannot move. What's wrong with my face? It feels all swollen, and it smarts dreadfully."

He tried to turn his head; but even with the effort his eyes seemed to grow glassy again, so I gently put it back. When he was quite conscious, he looked at me with an agonized confusion which I shall never forget, and said, "I must not deceive myself; it was no dream, but all a grim reality. Quick, Doctor, wet my lips with brandy. I have something that I must say before I die; or before my poor crushed brain dies anyhow. Thank you!

"It was that night after you left me, when I implored you to let me go away. I couldn't speak then, for I felt my tongue was tied; but I was as sane then, except in that way, as I am now. I was in an agony of despair for a long time after you left me; it seemed hours. Then there came a sudden peace to me. My brain seemed to become cool again, and I realized where I was. I heard the dogs bark behind our house, but not where He was!"

As he spoke Van Helsing's eyes never blinked, but his hand came out and met mine and gripped it hard. He did not, however, betray himself; he nodded slightly, and said, "Go on," in a low voice.

Renfield proceeded: "He came up to the window in the mist, as I had seen him often before; but he was solid then – not a ghost, and his eyes were fierce like a man's when angry.

He was laughing with his red mouth; the sharp white teeth glinted in the moonlight when he turned to look back over the belt of trees, to where the dogs were barking.

"I wouldn't ask him to come in at first, though I knew he wanted to – just as he had wanted all along. Then he began promising me things – not in words but by doing them."

He was interrupted by a word from the Professor: "How?"

"By making them happen; just as he used to send in the flies when the sun was shining. He beckoned me to the window, and He raised his hands, and seemed to call out without using any words. A dark mass spread over the grass, coming on like the shape of a flame of fire, and I could see that there were thousands of rats with their eyes blazing red – like His, only smaller.

"He held up his hand, and they all stopped; and I thought He seemed to be saying, 'All these lives will I give you, ay, and many more and greater, through countless ages, if you will

257

fall down and worship me!' And then a red cloud, like the colour of blood, seemed to close over my eyes; and before I knew what I was doing, I found myself opening the sash and saying to Him, 'Come in, Lord and Master!'"

His voice was weaker, so I moistened his lips with the brandy again, and he continued; but it seemed as though his memory had gone on working in the interval for his story was further advanced.

"All day I waited to hear from him, but he did not send me anything, not even a blow-fly, and when the moon got up I was pretty angry with him. When he slid in through the window, he sneered at me, and went on as though I was no one. He didn't even smell the same; I thought that, somehow, Mrs Harker had come into the room."

The Professor started and quivered; his face, however, grew grimmer and sterner still. Renfield went on without noticing:

"When Mrs Harker came in to see me this afternoon she wasn't the same; it was like tea after the teapot had been watered." Here we all moved, but no one said a word; he went on:

"I didn't know that she was here till she spoke; and she didn't look the same. When she went away I began to think, and it made me mad to know that He had been taking the life out of her. So when He came tonight I was ready for Him. I saw the mist stealing in, and I grabbed it tight. I had heard that madmen have unnatural strength, and I resolved to use my power.

"He raised me up and flung me down. There was a red cloud before me, and a noise like thunder, and the mist seemed to steal away under the door."

His voice was becoming fainter and his breath more stertorous. Van Helsing stood up instinctively.

"We know the worst now," he said. "He is here, and we know his purpose. It may not be too late. Let us be armed – the same as we were the other night, but lose no time; there is not an instant to spare."

We all hurried and took from our rooms the same things that we had when we entered the Count's house, and we met in the corridor.

Outside the Harkers' door we paused. Art and Quincey held back, and the latter said, "Should we disturb her?"

"We must," said Van Helsing grimly. "If the door be locked, I shall break it in."

He turned the handle as he spoke, but the door did not yield. We threw ourselves against it; with a crash it burst open, and we almost fell headlong into the room. What I saw appalled me. I felt my hair rise like bristles on the back of my neck, and my heart seemed to stand still.

# 6

# The Marriage Bed

What Seward saw, with his horrified companions, was the raw exchange of blood by which Dracula wrought his seductive evil. Wilhelmina Harker was in bed with her husband but her face was buried in the bare and bloody breast of "a tall, thin man, clad in black."

Jonathan appeared to be unconscious, or at least in some form of stupor, and his bride was kneeling on the marriage bed, facing outwards.

"Her white nightdress," Seward confided to his diary, "was smeared with blood, and a thin stream trickled down the man's bare breast. The attitude of the two had a terrible resemblance to a child forcing a kitten's nose into a saucer of milk to compel it to drink."

As the men burst in, the Count tore Mina's mouth from off his bleeding flesh, and threw her violently backwards across the bed. Then, clamping together the lips of his own "blood-dripping mouth", he sprang at them.

Van Helsing, then the others, halted him with their crucifixes and Sacred Wafer, and Dracula turned into vapour, to disappear beneath the bedroom door. Arthur and Quincey left in pursuit, but reported only that a bat had risen from Renfield's window and flapped westward – not to Carfax, but some other lair.

Before escaping, though, Dracula had gone to settle up the score with Renfield. This time there was no mistake: the zoo-phagous seeker of eternal life – was dead.

The state of Mina was pitiful. Thrown off by Dracula, she had released a scream of agony and despair that Seward thought would "ring in my ears till my dying day". Her face, he added, "was ghastly, with a pallor which was accentuated by the blood which smeared her lips and cheeks and chin; from her throat trickled a thin stream; her eyes were mad with terror."

Jonathan, when they aroused him, veered between wild rage and grief, which was surely deepened by the stains on his own night garment made by his wife's bloody mouth – the blood that she had sucked from Dracula. It was some long time before Mina, brave though she was, was capable of telling them her story.

She had, Dr Seward recorded, taken the sleeping draught that he had given her, and had not been wakened when her husband joined her in the bed. Some time later, though, she did awake – to find a thin white mist inside the room. This time it was Jonathan who would not wake, which filled her with a certain fear – that turned to terror when a tall, thin man appeared beside the bed.

"I knew him at once from the description of the others," *(she recounted, as recorded in the doctor's journal).* "For an instant my heart stood still, and I would have screamed out, only that I was paralysed. He spoke in a sort of keen, cutting whisper, pointing to Jonathan.

"'Silence! If you make a sound I shall take him and dash his brains out before your very eyes.' I was appalled and was too bewildered to do or say anything. With a mocking smile, he placed one hand upon my shoulder and, holding me tight, bared my throat with the other, saying as he did so, 'First, a little refreshment to reward my exertions.

"'You may as well be quiet; it is not the first time, or the second, that your veins have appeased my thirst!'

"I was bewildered, and, strangely enough, I did not want to hinder him. I suppose it is a part of the horrible curse. And oh, my God, my God, pity me! He placed his reeking lips upon my throat!"

*Her husband groaned again, Seward recorded, and she clasped his hand harder, and looked at him pityingly, as if he were the injured one, and went on,* "I felt my strength fading away, and I was in a half swoon. How long this horrible thing lasted I know not; but it seemed that a long time must have passed before he took his foul, awful, sneering mouth away.

"I saw it drip with the fresh blood! Then he spoke to me mockingly, 'And so you, like the others, would play your brains against mine. You would help these men to hunt me and frustrate me in my designs! You know now, and they know in part already, and will know in full before long, what it is to cross my path. They should have kept their energies for use closer to home.

"'Whilst they played wits against me – against me who commanded nations, and intrigued for them, and fought for them, hundreds of years before they were born – I was countermining them. And you, their best beloved one, are now to me, flesh of my flesh; blood of my blood; kin of my kin; my bountiful wine-press for a while; and shall be later on my companion and my helper.

"'But as yet you are to be punished for what you have done. You have aided in thwarting me; now you shall come to my call. When my brain says "Come!" to you, you shall cross land or sea to do my bidding; and to that end this!'

"With that he pulled open his shirt, and with his long sharp nails opened a vein in his breast. When the blood began to spurt out, he took my hands in one of his, holding them tight, and with the other seized my neck and pressed my mouth to the wound, so that I must either suffocate or swallow some of the—

"Oh my God! My God! What have I done? What have I done to deserve such a fate, I who have tried to walk in meekness and righteousness all my days. God pity me! Look down on a poor soul in worse than mortal peril; and in mercy pity those to whom she is dear!"

*Seward's diary concluded:* As she was telling her terrible story, the eastern sky began to quicken, and everything became more and more clear. Harker was still and quiet; but over his face, as the awful narrative went on, came a grey look which deepened and deepened in the morning light, till when the first red streak of the coming dawn shot up, the flesh stood darkly out against the whitening hair.

We have arranged that one of us is to stay within call of the unhappy pair till we can meet together and arrange about taking action.

Of this I am sure: the sun rises today on no more miserable house in all the great round of its daily course.

# 7

# The Mark of Shame

## Jonathan Harker's Journal

*3 October* – As I must do something or go mad, I write this diary. It is now six o'clock, and we are to meet in the study in half an hour and take something to eat; for Dr Van Helsing and Dr Seward are agreed that if we do not eat we cannot work our best. Our best will be, God knows, required today.

Poor Mina told me just now, with the tears running down her dear cheeks, that it is in trouble and trial that our faith is tested – that we must keep on trusting; and that God will aid us up to the end. The end! Oh my God! What end? … To work! To work!

When the question began to be discussed as to what should be our next step, the very first thing we decided was that Mina should be in full confidence; that nothing of any sort – no matter how painful – should be kept from her. She herself agreed as to its wisdom, and it was pitiful to see her so brave and yet so sorrowful, and in such a depth of despair.

Van Helsing said, suddenly but quietly, "But dear Madam Mina are you not afraid; not for yourself, but for others from yourself, after what has happened?"

Her face grew set in its lines, but her eyes shone with the devotion of a martyr as she answered, "Ah no! For my mind is made up!"

"To what?" he asked gently, whilst we were all very still; for each in our own way we had a sort of vague idea of what she meant.

"Because if I find in myself a sign of harm to any that I love, I shall die!"

"You would not kill yourself?" he asked, hoarsely.

"I would; if there were no friend who loved me, who would save me such a pain, and so desperate an effort!"

For a moment he seemed choked, and a great sob rose in his throat; he gulped it down and went on, "There are here some who would stand between you and death. You must not die. You must not die by any hand; but least of all by your own. Until the other, who has fouled your sweet life, is true dead you must not die; for if he is still with the quick Un-Dead, your death would make you even as he is.

"No, you must live! You must struggle and strive to live, though death would seem a boon unspeakable. You must fight Death himself, though he come to you in pain or in joy; by the day, or the night; in safety or in peril! On your living soul I charge you that you do not die – nay, nor think of death – till this great evil be past."

The poor dear grew white as death, and shook and shivered, as I have seen a quicksand shake and shiver at the incoming of the tide. We were all silent; we could do nothing. At length she grew more calm and turning to him said, "I promise you, my dear friend, that if God will let me live, I shall strive to do so; till, if it may be in His good time, this horror may have passed away from me."

She was so good and brave that we all felt that our hearts were strengthened to work and endure for her, and we began to discuss what we were to do.

As usual Van Helsing had thought ahead of everyone else, and was prepared with an exact ordering of our work.

"It is perhaps well," he said, "that after our visit to Carfax we decided not to do anything with the earth boxes that lay there. Had we done so, the Count must have guessed our purpose, and would doubtless have taken measures in advance to frustrate such an effort with regard to the others; but now he does not know our intentions.

"Today, then, is ours; and in it rests our hope. The sun that rose on our sorrow this morning guards us in its course. Until it sets tonight, that monster must retain whatever form he now has. He cannot melt into thin air nor disappear through cracks or chinks or crannies. If he go through a doorway, he must open the door like a mortal. And so we have this day to hunt out all his lairs and sterilize them."

Here I started up, for I could not contain myself. But Van Helsing held up his hand warningly.

"Friend Jonathan," he said, "in all probable the key of the situation is in that house in Piccadilly. The Count will have deeds of purchase, keys and other things: why not in this place so central, so quiet, where he come and go by the front or the back at all hour, when in the very vast of the traffic there is none to notice?

"We shall go there and search that house; and when we learn what it holds, then some of us can remain there whilst the rest find the other places where there be more earth boxes – at Bermondsey and Mile End."

Mina took a growing interest in everything, and I was rejoiced to see that the exigency of affairs was helping her to forget for a time the terrible experience of the night. She was very, very pale – almost ghastly, and so thin that her lips were drawn away, showing her teeth in somewhat of prominence; it made my blood run cold to think of what had occurred with poor Lucy when the Count had sucked her blood. As yet there was no sign of the teeth growing sharper; but the time as yet was short, and there was time for fear.

When we came to the discussion of the sequence of our efforts, there were new sources of doubt. It was finally agreed that before starting for Piccadilly we should destroy the Count's lair close at hand. I started up crying out, "In God's name, we are losing time. The Count may come to Piccadilly earlier than we think."

"Not so!" said Van Helsing, holding up his hand.

"But why?" I asked.

"Do you forget," he said, with actually a smile, "that last night he banqueted heavily, and will sleep late?"

Mina struggled hard to keep her brave countenance; but the pain overmastered her and she put her hands before her face, and shuddered whilst she moaned. Van Helsing, when it struck him what he had said, was horrified at his thoughtlessness.

"Oh Madam Mina," he said, "dear, dear, Madam Mina! Alas that I of all who so reverence you should have said anything so forgetful. These stupid old lips of mine and this stupid old head do not deserve so; but you will forget it, will you not?"

He bent low beside her as he spoke; she took his hand, and looking at him through her tears, said hoarsely, "No, I shall not forget, for it is well that I remember; and with it I have so much in memory of you that is sweet, that I take it all together. Now, you must all be going soon. Breakfast is ready, and we must all eat that we may be strong."

Breakfast was a strange meal to us all. We tried to be cheerful and encourage each other, and Mina was the brightest and most cheerful.

When it was over, Van Helsing stood up and said, "Now, my dear friends, we go forth to our terrible enterprise.

Madam Mina, before we go let me see you armed against personal attack. On your forehead I touch this piece of Sacred Wafer in the name of the Father, the Son, and—"

There was a fearful scream which almost froze our hearts to hear. As he had placed the Wafer on Mina's forehead, it had seared it – had burned into the flesh as though it had been a piece of white-hot metal. Pulling her beautiful hair over her face, as the leper of old his mantle, she wailed out, "Unclean! Unclean! Even the Almighty shuns my polluted flesh! I must bear this mark of shame upon my forehead until the Judgment Day."

All paused. I had thrown myself beside her in an agony of helpless grief, and putting my arms around, held her tight. For a few minutes our sorrowful hearts beat together, whilst the friends around us turned away their eyes that ran tears silently.

Then without a word we all knelt down together, and, all holding hands, swore to be true to each other. We men pledged ourselves to raise the veil of sorrow from the head of her whom, each in his own way, we loved; and we prayed for help and guidance in the terrible task which lay before us.

We entered Carfax without trouble and found all things the same as on the first occasion. Dr Van Helsing said to us, "And now, my friends, we have a duty here to do. He has chosen this earth because it has been holy. Thus we defeat him with his own weapon, for we make it more holy still. It was sanctified to such use of man, now we sanctify it to God."

As he spoke he took from his bag a screwdriver and a wrench, and very soon the top of one of the cases was thrown open. Taking from his box a piece of the Sacred Wafer he laid it reverently on the earth, and then shutting down the lid began to screw it home, we aiding him as he worked.

One by one we treated in the same way each of the great boxes, and left them as we had found them to all appearance; but in each was a portion of the Host.

When we closed the door behind us, the Professor said solemnly, "So much is already done. If it may be that with all the others we can be so successful, then the sunset of this evening may shine on Madam Mina's forehead all white as ivory and with no stain!"

As we passed across the lawn on our way to the station, we could see the front of the asylum. I looked eagerly, and in the window of my own room saw Mina, waving her hand in farewell. It was with a heavy heart that we caught the train, which was steaming in as we reached the platform. I have written this in the train.

*They reached the house in Piccadilly at half past midday, and used a locksmith to gain their illegal entry. Their thinking was that if two respectable men – Lord Godalming and Quincey Morris – stood watching while a hired workman did a job for them, no suspicions would be aroused. What's more, as Godalming put it, "My title will make it all right with any policeman that may come along." Indeed, not a soul took the slightest notice of the whole transaction. Van Helsing, Jonathan and Seward watched from some short distance.*

## Jonathan Harker's Journal

When the man had fairly gone, we three crossed the street and knocked at the door. It was immediately opened by Quincey Morris, beside whom stood Lord Godalming lighting a cigar. We moved to explore, all keeping together in case of attack; for as yet we did not know whether the Count might not be in the house.

In the dining-room, which lay at the back of the hall, we found eight boxes of earth. Eight boxes only out of the nine which we sought! Our work was not over, and would never be until we should have found the missing box.

First we opened the shutters of the window which looked out across a narrow stone-flagged yard at the blank face of a stable. There were no windows in it, so we were not afraid of being overlooked. We did not lose any time in examining the chests. With the tools which we had brought with us we opened them, one by one, and treated them as we had treated those others in the old chapel.

After a cursory glance at the rest of the rooms, from basement to attic, we came to the conclusion that the dining-room contained any effects which might belong to the Count; and so we proceeded to minutely examine them. They lay in a sort of orderly disorder on the table.

There were title deeds of the Piccadilly house in a great bundle; deeds of the purchase of the houses at Mile End and Bermondsey; notepaper, envelopes, and pens and ink. There were also a clothes brush, a brush and comb, and a basin containing dirty water which was reddened as if with blood. Last of all was a heap of keys.

When we had examined this last find, Lord Godalming and Quincey Morris, taking accurate notes of the various addresses of the houses in the East and the South, took with them the keys in a great bunch, and set out to destroy the boxes in these places.

The rest of us are, with what patience we can, awaiting their return.

Or – the coming of the Count.

# 8

# *Failure*

*The long wait for Godalming and Morris to return was chron-icled by Dr Seward. Van Helsing tried to keep them cheerful, but with an air of desperation rather than of full-blown hope. And although Harker's energy was "intact", Seward noted that he was overwhelmed by appalling misery.*

*"Last night" (wrote Seward), "he was a frank, happy-looking man, with strong, youthful face and dark brown hair. Today he is a drawn, haggard old man, whose white hair matches well with the hollow burning eyes and grief-written lines of his face."*

*Mina, still active although safe at the asylum, gave them their first fright, in the form of an unexpected knocking at the door – by a telegraph boy. Her telegram reported that Dracula had left Carfax "hurriedly", and was heading towards London. But half an hour later a second, different knock – "such as is given by gentlemen" – revealed Godalming and Quincey on the step.*

*   *   *

## Dr Seward's Diary

*3 October* – They came quickly in and closed the door behind them, the former saying, as they moved along the hall, "It is all right. We found both places; six boxes in each, and we destroyed them all!"

"Destroyed?" asked the Professor.

"For him!" We were silent for a minute, and then Quincey said, "There's nothing to do but to wait here. If, however, he doesn't turn up by five o'clock, we must start off; for it won't do to leave Mrs Harker alone after sunset."

"He will be here before long now," said Van Helsing. "*Nota bene*, in Madam's telegram he went south from Carfax, that means he went to cross the river. Believe me, my friends, we shall not have long to wait. We should have ready some plan of attack, so that we may throw away no chance.

"Hush, there is no time now. Have all your arms! Be ready!" He held up a warning hand as he spoke, for we all could hear a key softly inserted in the lock of the hall door.

I could not but admire, even at such a moment, the way in which a dominant spirit asserted itself. Quincey Morris, without speaking a word, with a gesture placed us each in position. We waited in a suspense that made the seconds pass with nightmare slowness. The slow, careful steps came along the hall; the Count was evidently prepared for some surprise – at least he feared it.

Suddenly with a single bound he leaped into the room,

winning a way past us before any of us could raise a hand to stay him. There was something so panther-like in the movement – something so unhuman – that it seemed to sober us all from the shock of his coming.

As the Count saw us, a horrible sort of snarl passed over his face, showing the eye-teeth long and pointed; but the evil smile as quickly passed into a cold stare of lion-like disdain.

Harker evidently meant to try the matter, for he had ready his great Kukri knife, and made a fierce and sudden cut at him. The blow was a powerful one; only the diabolical quickness of the Count's leap back saved him. A second less and the trenchant blade had shorne through his heart.

As it was, the point just cut the cloth of his coat, making a wide gap whence a bundle of banknotes and a stream of gold fell out. The expression of the Count's face was so hellish, that for a moment I feared for Harker, though I saw him throw the terrible knife aloft again for another stroke.

Instinctively I moved forward with a protective impulse, holding the crucifix and wafer in my left hand. I felt a mighty power fly along my arm; and it was without surprise that I saw the monster cower back before a similar movement made spontaneously by each one of us.

It would be impossible to describe the expression of hate and baffled malignity – of anger and hellish rage – which came over the Count's face. His waxen hue became greenish-yellow by the contrast of his burning eyes, and the red scar

on the forehead showed on the pallid skin like a palpitating wound.

The next instant, with a sinuous dive he swept under Harker's arm, ere his blow could fall, and, grasping a handful of the money from the floor, dashed across the room; and threw himself at the window.

Amid the crash and glitter of the falling glass, he tumbled into the flagged area below. Through the sound of the shivering glass I could hear the "ting" of the gold, as some of the sovereigns fell on the flagging.

We ran over and saw him spring unhurt from the ground. He, rushing up the steps, crossed the yard, and pushed open the stable door. There he turned and spoke to us:

"You think to baffle me, you – with your pale faces all in a row, like sheep in a butcher's. You shall be sorry yet, each one of you! You think you have left me without a place to rest; but I have more. My revenge is just begun! I spread it over centuries, and time is on my side.

"Your girls that you all love are mine already; and through them you and others shall yet be mine – my creatures, to do my bidding and to be my jackals when I want to feed. Bah!"

With a contemptuous sneer, he passed quickly through the door, and we heard the rusty bolt creak as he fastened it behind him. A door beyond opened and shut.

It was now late in the afternoon, and sunset was not far off. We had to recognize that our game was up; with heavy hearts we agreed with the Professor when he said, "Let us go back to Madam Mina. All we can do just now is done; and we can there, at least, protect her. There is but one more earth box, and we must try to find it; when that is done all may yet be well."

Jonathan was "quite broken down" with their failure, Seward recorded, because of the effect the bad news would have on Mina. When they returned to the asylum, though, they found that she was made of sterner stuff.

## Dr Seward's Diary

With sad hearts we came back to my house, where we found Mrs Harker awaiting us, with an appearance of cheerfulness which did honour to her bravery and unselfishness. When she saw our faces, her own became as pale as death; for a second or two her eyes were closed as if she were in secret prayer.

And then she said cheerfully, "I can never thank you all enough. Oh, my poor darling!" She took her husband's grey head in her hands and kissed it. "All will yet be well, dear! God will protect us if He so will it in His good intent." The poor fellow only groaned. There was no place for words in his sublime misery.

We had a sort of perfunctory supper together, and I think it cheered us all up somewhat. True to our promise, we told Mrs Harker everything which had passed; and although she grew snowy white at times, she listened bravely and with calmness. Then without letting go her husband's hand she stood up amongst us and spoke.

"Jonathan," she said, "Jonathan dear, and you all, my true, true friends, I want you to bear something in mind through all this dreadful time.

"I know that you must fight – that you must destroy even as you destroyed the false Lucy so that the true Lucy might live hereafter; but it is not a work of hate.

"That poor soul who has wrought all this misery is the

saddest case of all. Just think what will be his joy when he too is destroyed in his worser part that his better part may have spiritual immortality. You must be pitiful to him too, though it may not hold your hands from his destruction."

As she spoke I could see her husband's face darken and draw together, as though the passion in him were shrivelling his being to its core. Instinctively the clasp on his wife's hand grew closer, till his knuckles looked white. She did not flinch from the pain which I knew she must have suffered, but looked at him with eyes that were more appealing than ever.

As she stopped speaking he leaped to his feet, almost tearing his hand from hers as he spoke: "May God give him into my hand just for long enough to destroy that earthly life of him which we are aiming at. If beyond it I could send his soul for ever and ever to burning hell I would do it!"

"Oh, hush! Oh, hush! In the name of the good God. Don't say such things, Jonathan, my husband; or you will crush me with fear and horror. Just think, my dear – I have been thinking all this long, long day of it – that ... perhaps ... some day ... I too may need such pity; and that some other like you – and with equal cause for anger – may deny it to me!

"Oh, my husband! I pray that God may not have treasured your wild words, except as the heartbroken wail of a sorely stricken man. Oh God, let these poor white hairs go in evidence of what he has suffered, who all his life has done no wrong, and on whom so many sorrows have come."

We men were all in tears now. There was no resisting them, and we wept openly. She wept too, to see that her sweeter counsels had prevailed. Her husband flung himself on his knees beside her, and putting his arms round her, hid his face in the folds of her dress.

Van Helsing beckoned to us and we stole out of the room, leaving the two loving hearts alone with their God.

### Jonathan Harker's Journal

*3-4 October, close to midnight* – I thought yesterday would never end. Before we parted, we discussed what our next step was to be, but we could arrive at no result. All we knew was that one earth box remained, and that the Count alone knew where it was.

If he chooses to lie hidden, he may baffle us for years; and in the meantime! – the thought is too horrible, I dare not think of it. We are all drifting reefwards now, and faith is our only anchor.

Thank God! Mina is sleeping, and sleeping without dreams. I am not sleepy myself, though I am weary to death. However, I must try to sleep; for there is tomorrow to think of, and there is no rest for me until...

*4 October, morning* – I must have fallen asleep, for I was awakened by Mina, who was sitting up in bed, with a startled look on her face. She said to me hurriedly, "Go, call the Professor. I want to see him at once."

"Why?" I asked.

"I have an idea. I suppose it must have come in the night, and matured without my knowing it. He must hypnotize me before the dawn, and then I shall be able to speak. Go quick, dearest; the time is getting close."

Two or three minutes later Van Helsing was in the room in his dressing-gown, and Mr Morris and Lord Godalming were with Dr Seward at the door.

"I want you to hypnotize me!" she said. "Do it before the dawn, for I feel that I can speak, and speak freely. Be quick, for the time is short!" Without a word he motioned her to sit up in bed.

Looking fixedly at her, he commenced to make passes from over the top of her head downward, with each hand in turn. Gradually her eyes closed, and she sat, stock still; only by the gentle heaving of her bosom could one know that she was alive.

The Professor made a few more passes, then Mina opened her eyes; but she did not seem the same woman. There was a faraway look in her eyes, and her voice had a sad dreaminess which was new to me. Raising his hand to impose silence, the Professor motioned to me to bring the others in. They came on tiptoe, closing the door behind them, and stood at the foot of the bed, looking on.

Mina appeared not to see them. The stillness was broken by Van Helsing's voice speaking in a low, level tone which would not break the current of her thoughts.

"Where are you?"

The answer came in a neutral way, "I do not know. Sleep has no place it can call its own." For several minutes there was silence. Mina sat rigid, and the Professor stood staring at her fixedly; the rest of us hardly dared to breathe.

The room was growing lighter; without taking his eyes from Mina's face, Dr Van Helsing motioned me to pull up the blind. I did so, and the day seemed just upon us. A red streak shot up, and a rosy light seemed to diffuse itself through the room. On the instant the Professor spoke again.

"Where are you now?"

The answer came dreamily, but with intention; it was as though she were interpreting something.

"I do not know. It is all strange to me!"

"What do you see?"

"I can see nothing; it is all dark."

"What do you hear?" I could detect the strain in the Professor's patient voice.

"The lapping of water. It is gurgling by, and little waves leap. I can hear them on the outside."

"Then you are on a ship?"

The answer came quick: "Oh, yes!"

"What else do you hear?"

"The sound of men stamping overhead as they run about. There is the creaking of a chain, and the loud tinkle as the check of the capstan falls into the ratchet."

"What are you doing?"

"I am still – oh, so still. It is like death!" The voice faded away into a deep breath as of one sleeping, and the open eyes closed again.

By this time the sun had risen, and we were all in the full light of day. Dr Van Helsing placed his hands on Mina's shoulders, and laid her head down softly on her pillow. She lay like a sleeping child for a few moments, and then, with a long sigh, awoke and stared in wonder to see us all around her.

"Have I been talking in my sleep?" was all she said. She seemed, however, to know the situation without telling; though she was eager to know what she had told. The Professor repeated the conversation, and she said, "Then there is not a moment to lose; it may not be yet too late!"

Mr Morris and Lord Godalming started for the door but the Professor's calm voice called them back.

"Stay, my friends. That ship, wherever it was, was weighing anchor whilst she spoke. There are many ships weighing anchor at the moment in your so great Port of London. Which of them is it that you seek? God be thanked that we have once again a clue, though whither it may lead us we know not.

"We can know now what was in the Count's mind when

he seize that money, though. He meant escape. Hear me, ESCAPE! He saw that with but one earth box left, and a pack of men following like dogs after a fox, this London was no place for him. He have take his last earth box on board a ship, and he leave the land. He think to escape, but no! We follow him. Tally Ho!

"In meantime we may rest and in peace, for there are waters between us which he do not want to pass, and which he could not if he would - unless the ship were to touch the land, and then only at full or slack tide.

"See, and the sun is just rose, and all day to sunset is to us. Let us take bath, and dress, and have breakfast which we all need, and which we can eat comfortable since he be not in the same land with us."

Mina looked at him appealingly as she asked, "But why need we seek him further, when he is gone away from us?"

He took her hand and patted it as he replied, "Ask me nothings as yet. When we have breakfast, then I answer all questions." He would say no more, and we separated to dress.

After breakfast Mina repeated her question. He looked at her gravely for a minute and then said sorrowfully, "Because my dear, dear Madam Mina, now more than ever must we find him even if we have to follow him to the jaws of Hell!"

She grew paler as she asked faintly, "Why?"

"Because," he answered solemnly, "he can live for centuries, and you are but mortal woman. Time is now to be dreaded – since once he put that mark upon you."

I was just in time to catch her as she fell forward in a faint.

*Book Five*

## THE JAWS
## of HELL

# 1

# A Burial Service

Van Helsing, by a combination of reasoning and good, hard cash, quickly discovered the ship on which Count Dracula's last crate of earth had been loaded. She was the Czarina Catherine, and had left London docks already, bound for the Black Sea port of Varna. The vampire, Un-Dead in his box, was clearly going "home".

Bribed with beer money from Quincey Morris's deep pockets, the workers at the docks reported that a tall, thin man with burning eyes had lifted the heavy box from off a cart unaided at the dockside – although it had taken several men to get it on the ship and stowed inside. Despite grave warnings that they were about to sail, he had refused to cross the gangplank himself to check the stowage, and had walked away. But to the captain's fury the ship could not depart, as suddenly a strange, thin mist had risen, preventing movement on the river.

The man had returned at full tide – when the water all around the hull was slack – and gone into the hold to check his

box. But although the mist had then quickly melted, he must
have left the ship again before it cleared, for no one had seen
him go. Strangely, no other ship in the vicinity had been fog-
bound. The phenomenon had been completely localized.

*Van Helsing's plan, when he'd recounted this, was that they should travel overland to Transylvania (which they could reach much sooner than the ship could) and meet her one day between dawn and sunset. They would then open the box – with the monster helpless – and "deal with him as we should."*

*But while Mina was easily convinced that they had to follow Dracula, others had their doubts. Over the next few days Jack Seward began to nurture fears about her – but hardly dared to voice them about such a "noble woman". Van Helsing, though, forestalled him.*

*"Friend John, there is something that you and I must talk of alone, just at the first at any rate. Later, we may have to take the others into our confidence."*

*He stopped, and Seward waited.*

*Van Helsing went on, "Madam Mina, our poor, dear Madam Mina, is changing."*

### Dr Seward's Diary

A cold shiver ran through me to find my worst fears thus endorsed. Van Helsing continued, "With the sad experience of Miss Lucy, we must this time be warned. I can see the characteristics of the vampire coming in her face. It is now but very, very slight; but it is to be seen if we have eyes to notice without prejudge. Her teeth are some sharper, and at times her eyes are more hard.

"My fear is this. If it be that she can, by our hypnotic

trance, tell what the Count see and hear, is it not more true that he who have hypnotize her first, and who have drink of her very blood and make her drink of his, should, if he will, compel her mind to disclose to him that which she know?"

I nodded acquiescence; he went on, "Then, what we must do is to prevent this; we must keep her ignorant of our intent, and so she cannot tell what she know not. This is a painful task! Oh! So painful that it heartbreak me to think of; but it must be. When today we meet, I must tell her she must not more be of our council, but be simply guarded by us."

He wiped his forehead, which had broken out in profuse perspiration at the thought of the pain which he might have to inflict upon the poor soul already so tortured. I knew that it would be some sort of comfort to him if I told him that I also had come to the same conclusion; for at any rate it would take away the pain of doubt. I told him, and the effect was as I expected.

*Later, though, Mina revealed the full depths of her own intelligence and understanding. She did not turn up for the scheduled meeting of the "council", sending a message via her husband that she knew her presence would "embarrass" them. The men, relieved, discussed tactics and supplies for the expedition – including Winchester repeating rifles for the "wolf country" they were going to. Then came a shock for Jonathan.*

*"Tonight and tomorrow," said Van Helsing, "we can get ready,*

and then, if all be well, we four can set out on our journey."

"We four?" said Harker.

"Of course!" answered the Professor quickly. "You must remain to take care of your so sweet wife!"

Even this edict Mina took in her stride, although Jonathan found it food for much deep thought. Then, suddenly, she changed her mind. On 6 October she called Van Helsing into her room, and told him, "You must take me with you. I am safer with you, and you shall be safer too."

Her reasoning was impeccable. Since the Master could call her, across sea and continent, at will, she was fated, cursed, to cheat and hoodwink all of them – including Jonathan – to do Dracula's bidding. They would therefore be safer if they always had her in their sight.

"Besides," she added. "I may be of service, since you can hypnotize me and so learn that which even I myself do not know."

As always, said Van Helsing, Madam Mina had proved herself most wise. And later, with her will of iron, she made them promise, one by one, that they would kill her if they needed to while on their journey, then "without a moment's delay, drive a stake through me and cut off my head."

Her husband turned to her – Dr Seward noted in his diary – wan-eyed and with a greenish pallor which subdued the snowy whiteness of his hair, and asked, "And must I, too, make such a promise?"

"You too, my dearest. You must not shrink. If it is to be that

I must meet death at any hand, let it be at the hand of him that loves me best."

Mina's last request was a chilling one. She asked the friends to kneel around her while her husband read the Burial Service as if she were already dead. "It would comfort me," was all she said, and once more she was right.

As Seward recorded: "How can I – how could anyone – tell of that strange scene, its solemnity, its gloom, its sadness, its horror; and, withal, its sweetness. Even a sceptic, who can see nothing but a travesty of bitter truth in anything holy or emotional, would have been melted to the heart had he seen that little group of loving and devoted friends kneeling round that stricken and sorrowing lady; or heard the tender passion of her husband's voice, as in tones so broken with emotion that often he had to pause, he read the simple and beautiful service for the Burial of the Dead."

And there, in broken words and stammering, his diary entry on the phonograph ... cut off.

# The Hunt Is Up

*They left, as Jonathan recorded in his journal, from Charing Cross Station, London, on the morning of 12 October. By the evening they were in Paris, where they took their pre-booked places on the Orient Express. Travelling night and day, they reached their destination, Varna, at about five o'clock in the afternoon of the fifteenth, when Lord Godalming went straight to the British Consulate to check for news of the Czarina Catherine. There was none.*

## Jonathan Harker's Journal

Thank God! Mina is well, and looks to be getting stronger;

her colour is coming back. She sleeps a great deal; throughout the journey she slept nearly all the time.

Before sunrise and sunset, however, she is very wakeful and alert; and it has become a habit for Van Helsing to hypnotize her at such times. At first, some effort was needed, and he had to make many passes; but now, she seems to yield at once, as if by habit, and scarcely any action is needed.

He always asks her what she can see and hear. She answers to the first: "Nothing; all is dark." And to the second: "I can hear the waves lapping against the ship, and the water rushing by."

*Godalming's agent, in London, was in touch with Lloyd's, the ship insurers, to keep track of the vessel by reported sightings and by signal stations, as was the way before radio had been invented. Van Helsing and Seward were in constant readiness to go on board and "cut off his head at once and drive a stake through his heart."*

*Harker added:* The Professor says that if we can so treat the Count's body, it will soon after fall into dust. In such case there would be no evidence against us, in case any suspicion of murder were aroused. But even if it were not so, we should stand or fall by our act, and perhaps some day this very script may be evidence to come between some of us and a rope.

For myself, I should take the chance only too thankfully if it were to come. We mean to leave no stone unturned to carry out our intent. We have arranged with certain officials that the instant the *Czarina Catherine* is seen, we are to be informed by a special messenger.

*That entry was dated 17 October, and the anxious days crept onward with no kind of news. Godalming received daily telegrams, but they contained "only the same story". Mina was put under each morning and evening, likewise – with the same hypnotic answer: lapping waves, rushing water, creaking masts...*

*And then, on 24 October, the message they had all been waiting for:*

CZARINA CATHERINE REPORTED THIS MORNING FROM DARDANELLES.

## Dr Seward's Diary

25 October – We were all wild with excitement yesterday when Godalming got his telegram from Lloyd's. I know now what men feel in battle when the call to action is heard.

Mrs Harker, alone of our party, did not show any signs of emotion. In this way she is greatly changed during the past three weeks. The lethargy grows upon her, and though she seems strong and well, Van Helsing and I are not satisfied. We have not, however, said a word to the others. It would break poor Harker's heart if he knew that we had even a suspicion on the subject.

It is only about 24 hours' sail from the Dardanelles to here, at the rate the *Czarina Catherine* has come from London. She should therefore arrive some time in the morning; but as she cannot possibly get in before then, we are all about to retire early. We shall get up at one o'clock, so as to be ready.

*Count Dracula, however, had hardly given up the fight so easily. By noon that day, despite Seward's confidence, the ship had not arrived. Nor had there been any sight or sound of her twenty-four hours later, although Mina's trance reported her, as usual, still at sea.*

*By 27 October, Van Helsing admitted to Seward that he feared that somehow, in some unfathomable way, the Count was getting free of them. The state of "Madam Mina" was also giving him concern. "Souls and memories," he said enigmatically, "can do strange things during trance."*

*Then – on the twenty-eighth – another telegram arrived, via the British Consulate. The* Czarina Catherine *had entered Galatz that day.*

*It was another port entirely. Count Dracula had given them the slip...*

# 3

# A Throat Torn Out

## Dr Seward's Diary

*28 October* – When the telegram came I do not think it was such a shock to any of us as might have been expected. True, we did not know whence, or how, or when, the bolt would come; but I think we all expected that something strange would happen.

It was an odd experience, and we all took it differently. Van Helsing raised his hands over his head for a moment, as though in remonstrance with the Almighty; but he said not a word, and in a few seconds stood up with his face sternly set.

Mrs Harker grew ghastly white, so that the scar on her forehead seemed to burn, but she folded her hands meekly and looked up in prayer. Harker smiled – actually smiled – the dark bitter smile of one who is without hope; but at the same time his action belied his words, for his hands instinctively sought the hilt of the great Kukri knife and rested there.

"When does the next train start for Galatz?" said Van Helsing to us generally.

"At 6.30 tomorrow morning."

We all stared, for the answer came from Mrs Harker.

"How on earth do you know?" said Art.

"You forget – or perhaps you do not know – that I am the train fiend. At home in Exeter I always used to make up the timetables, so as to be helpful to my husband. I knew that if anything were to take us to Castle Dracula we should go by Galatz, or at any rate through Bucharest, so I learned the times very carefully. Unhappily there are not many to learn, as the only train tomorrow leaves as I say."

"Wonderful woman!" murmured the Professor.


*Even in Galatz, though, which they reached on the morning of 30 October, Dracula had both avoided their clutches – he had already left the ship – and taken care to cover up his tracks.*

*They learned from the captain of the* Czarina Catherine *the name of the agent, Immanuel Hildesheim, who had arrived at the ship before sunrise on the morning she had docked, with an order from England authorizing the removal of the box. Hildesheim, traced to his office, reported that he had put it in the charge of a certain Petrof Skinsky, who had taken it away.*

*What Skinsky had done with it, however, Dracula intended to remain unknowable, unknown. For when they sought him out, they heard only that he had been murdered. Jonathan*

*Harker wrote in his journal:* One of his neighbours, who did not seem to bear him any affection, said that he had gone away two days before, no one knew whither. This was corroborated by his landlord.

Whilst we were talking, one came running and breathlessly gasped out that the body of Skinsky had been found inside the wall of the churchyard of St Peter, and that the throat had been torn open as if by some wild animal.

Those we had been speaking with ran off to see the horror, the women crying out "This is the work of a Slovak!" We hurried away lest we should have been in some way drawn into the affair, and so detained.

As we came home we could arrive at no definite conclusion. We were all convinced that the box was on its way to somewhere; but where that might be we would have to discover. With heavy hearts we came home to the hotel to Mina.

*It was an inspired decision, as it turned out. Noting that the men were all "worn out and dispirited" and in desperate need of rest, Mina took it on herself to try and enter the thought-processes of her mortal enemy – "without prejudice on the facts before me." His problem, as she saw it, was to get back to his castle, where he could be safe, with the proviso that he could not achieve it on his own.*

*As she expressed it in her journal, "He must be brought back by someone. This is evident; for had he power to move himself as* he wished he could go either as man, or wolf, or bat, or in some other way. He evidently fears discovery or interference, in the state of helplessness in which he must be – confined as he is between dawn and sunset in his wooden box."

Mina then considered the transport possibilities, ruling them out as she listed the difficulties. Road was the worst, quite obviously. There were people, for a start – curious people, who would investigate. Then there were Customs posts, and other controls, with their attendant dangers. Finally – "His pursuers might follow. This is his greatest fear."

Railways, she considered, were little better. For a start, there would be no one "in charge" of the box, and delays were eminently likely in this part of the world – which would give his enemies time to catch him up. He might escape at night, she added, but "What would he be, if left in a strange place with no refuge he could fly to?"

Which left only water, which was at once least dangerous, and most. The road and railway problems would be solved, but if he were wrecked, and the waters engulfed him, "He would indeed be lost." However, Dracula had achieved much by water so far, and the last time she had linked with him hypnotically he had been on water still. What is more, Mina surmised, he had laid his plans out in London before he had even left, and so far they had worked superbly.

In a memorandum, she laid out her conclusions for the men's consideration:

My surmise is this: that in London the Count decided to get back to his Castle by water, as the most safe and secret way. He was brought from the Castle by Szgany, and thus had knowledge of the persons who could arrange this service.

When the box was on land, before sunrise or after sunset, he came out, met Skinsky and instructed him what to do as to arranging the carriage of the box up some river. When this was done, he blotted out his traces – as he thought – by murdering his agent.

I have examined the map and find that the river most suitable is either the Pruth or the Sereth. Of these two, the Pruth is the more easily navigated, but the Sereth is, at Fundu, joined by the Bistritza, which runs up round the Borgo Pass. The loop it makes is manifestly as close to Dracula's Castle as can be got by water.

*Mina, when she read this out to the five men, was overwhelmed by their response. Jonathan took her in his arms and kissed her, while the others shook her "by both hands" and brimmed over with admiration. Within minutes the outline of their strategy was agreed. Lord Godalming and Jonathan were to obtain a steam launch and set out up the Sereth, Morris and Seward were to follow the river bank on horseback, in case the Count should come to shore, while Mina and Van Helsing...*

*It was here that implications raised their heads; and problems had to be confronted. If Jonathan went with Arthur, he could not protect his wife. And what, exactly, did the Professor have in mind for Mina and himself?*

## Mina Harker's Journal

Jonathan looked at me. I could see that the poor dear was torn about in his mind. During his silence Dr Van Helsing spoke: "Friend Jonathan, be not afraid for Madam Mina. I am old, but I can be of other service; I can fight in other way. And I can die, if need be, as well as younger men.

"While you go in your so swift little steamboat up the river, and whilst John and Quincey guard the bank, I will take Madam Mina right into the heart of the enemy's country. Whilst the old fox is tied in his box, floating on the running stream whence he cannot escape to land, we shall go from Bistritz over the Borgo, and find our way to the Castle of Dracula. There is much to be done, and other places to be made sanctify, so that that nest of vipers be obliterated."

Here Jonathan interrupted him hotly.

"Do you mean to say, Professor Van Helsing, that you would bring Mina, in her sad case and tainted as she is with that devil's illness, right into the jaws of his death-trap? Not for the world! Not for Heaven or Hell!"

He became almost speechless for a minute, and then went on, "Do you know what the place is? Have you seen that awful den of hellish infamy – with the very moonlight alive with grisly shapes, and every speck of dust that whirls in the wind a devouring monster in embryo? Have you felt the Vampire's lips upon your throat?"

Here he turned to me, and as his eyes lit on my forehead, he threw up his arms with a cry: "Oh, my God, what have we done to have this terror upon us!" And he sank down on the sofa in a collapse of misery.

The Professor's voice, as he spoke in clear, sweet tones, which seemed to vibrate in the air, calmed us all.

"Oh my friend, it is because I would save Madam Mina from that awful place that I would go. God forbid that I should take her into that place. There is work - wild work - to be done there, that her eyes may not see.

"If the Count escape us this time, he may choose to sleep him for a century. And then in time our dear one" - he took my hand - "would come to him to keep him company, and would be as those others that you saw.

"You have told us of their gloating lips; you heard their ribald laugh as they clutched the moving bag that the Count threw to them. You shudder; and well may it be. Is it not a dire need for the which I am giving, if need be, my life?"

"Do as you will," said Jonathan, with a sob that shook him all over, "we are in the hands of God!"

# 4

# The Wild Adventure

The last, and desperate, journey started that very evening. Jonathan Harker's next journal entry was written by the light cast through the open furnace door of the steam launch Godalming had hired, as they rushed through the quiet darkness of the Sereth river. Quincey Morris and Seward had set off on their horses before the launch had raised sufficient steam, while Mina and Professor Van Helsing caught the train for Veresti at almost midnight. All were armed and hopeful; all eyes were peeled. It was to be six days before they would meet again.

Travel in those far-off days – even given steam trains and launches – was extremely hard. Mina and Van Helsing reached Veresti in twelve hours, which left them only about seventy miles short of their final destination. This, however, meant the searching out and purchasing of a sturdy carriage, and the first of many horses, to be "changed" along the route.

They also needed, Mina wrote, a basket of provisions, and a "wonderful" lot of fur coats and blankets to save them from the *cold. She found the people on the way "full of nice qualities", although "very, very superstitious".*

*She noted: "In the first house where we stopped, when the woman who served us saw the scar on my forehead, she crossed herself and put out two fingers towards me, to keep off the evil eye. Ever since then I have taken care not to take off my hat or veil, and so have escaped their suspicions."*

*The drive, although long and gruelling, passed off without mishap. Because Van Helsing looked so old and tired, Mina insisted that she share the driving, to keep their strengths up. She was hypnotized when possible, but reported only darkness, creaking wood and water.*

*To her there still seemed room for hope. The Professor, before much longer, secretly appeared to hold a bleaker view.*

### *Memorandum by Abraham Van Helsing*

4 November – This to my old and true friend John Seward, MD, of Purfleet, London, in case I may not see him. It may explain.

It is morning, and I write by a fire which all the night I have kept alive. It is cold, cold; so cold that the grey heavy sky is full of snow, which when it falls will settle for all winter as the ground is hardening to receive it.

It seems to have affected Madam Mina; she sleeps, and sleeps, and sleeps! She, who is usual so alert, have done literally nothing all the day; she even have lost her appetite. She make no entry into her little diary, she who write so faithful at every pause. Something whisper to me that all is not well.

At sunset I try to hypnotize her, but alas! with no effect; the power has grown less and less with each day, and tonight it fail me altogether. Well, God's will be done – whatever it may be, and whithersoever it may lead!

We got to the Borgo Pass just after sunrise yesterday morning. At this time and place she become all on fire with zeal; some new guiding power be in her manifested, for she point to a road and say, "This is the way."

"How know you it?" I ask.

"Of course I know it," she answer, and with a pause add, "Have not my Jonathan travel and wrote of his travel?"

I think somewhat strange, but we come down this road. When we meet other ways – not always sure that they were roads at all, for snow have fallen – the horses know and they only. I give rein to them, and they go on so patient for long, long hours.

At the first, I tell Madam Mina to sleep; she try, and she succeed. She sleep all the time; till at the last, I feel myself to suspicious grow, and attempt to wake her. But she sleep on, and I may not wake her though I try.

I think I drowse myself, for all of sudden I feel guilt, as though I have done something. It is now not far off sunset time, and over the snow the light of the sun flow in big yellow flood, so that we throw great long shadow on where the mountain rise so steep. For we are going up, and up; and all is oh! so wild and rocky, as though it were the end of the world.

Then I arouse Madam Mina. This time she wake with not much trouble, and then I try to put her to hypnotic sleep – but she sleep not. Still I try and try, till all at once I find her and myself in dark; so I look round, and find that the sun have gone down. Madam Mina laugh, and I turn and look at her.

She is now quite awake, and look so well as I never saw her since that night at Carfax when we first enter the Count's house. I am amaze, and not at ease then; but she is so bright and tender and thoughtful for me that I forget all fear.

I light a fire, and she prepare food while I undo the horses and set them, tethered in shelter, to feed. Then when I return to the fire she have my supper ready. I go to help her; but she smile, and tell me that she have eat already – that she was so hungry that she would not wait. I like it not, and I have grave doubts; but I fear to affright her, and so I am silent of it.

I eat alone; and then we wrap in fur and lie beside the fire, and I tell her to sleep while I watch. But presently I forget all of watching; and when I sudden remember that I watch, I find her lying quiet, but awake, and looking at me with so bright eyes. Once, twice more the same occur, and I get much sleep till before morning.

When I wake I try to hypnotize her; but alas! Though she shut her eyes obedient, she may not sleep. The sun rise up, and up, and up; and then sleep come to her too late, but so heavy that she will not wake. I have to lift her up, and place her sleeping in the carriage when I have harnessed the horses and made all ready.

Madam still sleep, and sleep; and she look in her sleep more healthy and more redder than before. And I like it not. And I am afraid, afraid, afraid!

I am afraid of all things – even to think; but I must go on my way. The stake we play for is life and death, or more than these, and we must not flinch.

*Had Van Helsing known the difficulties the others were facing, he would perhaps have been even more pessimistic. Godalming and Harker had made good speed, but had had neither firm intelligence nor any sightings of the enemy. And on 4 November, while trying to force a way up a set of rapids, their boat had been damaged in an accident.*

*Repairs were done, but they had lost many hours. What was worse, the boat was no longer to be relied upon. They abandoned her and hired horses. Jonathan was almost in despair.*

5

# The Evil Sisters

By the time Van Helsing continued his "farewell memorandum" to Dr Seward, he had seen things and undergone things that made him fear, genuinely, that he had become insane. He was beset with growing terror that Mina was succumbing to "the fatal spell" of Castle Dracula as they got nearer. He had once again been unable to rouse her, and once again been incapable of keeping watch without falling asleep.

The stolid horses had plodded on, however, and when he awoke again he realized that they were very near the end of their journey. There was a castle visible – "such a castle as

*Jonathan tells of in his journal" – which made him at once*
*exultant and full of fear. He did wake Mina now, although he*
*failed to hypnotize her, and then made some hurried prepara-*
*tions before the "great dark" came upon them. The change in her*
*frightened him.*

## Memorandum by Abraham Van Helsing

5 November, morning – I took out the horses and fed them in
what shelter I could. Then I make a fire; and near it I make
Madam Mina sit comfortable amid her rugs. I got ready food:
but she would not eat, simply saying that she had not hunger.
I did not press her, knowing her unavailingness. But I myself
eat, for I must needs now be strong for all.

Then, with the fear on me of what might be, I drew a ring
round where Madam Mina sat; and over the ring I passed some
of the Wafer, and I broke it fine so that all was well guarded.

She sat still all the time - so still as one dead; and she grew
whiter and ever whiter till the snow was not more pale; and
no word she said. But when I drew near, she clung to me, and
I could know that the poor soul shook her from head to feet
with a tremor that was pain to feel.

I said to her presently, when she had grown more quiet,
"Will you not come over to the fire?" for I wished to make a
test of what she could. She rose obedient, but when she then
made a step she stopped, and stood as one stricken.

"Why not go on?" I asked. She shook her head, and,

coming back, sat down in her place. Then, looking at me with open eyes, as of one waked from sleep, she said simply, "I cannot!" and remained silent.

I rejoiced, for I knew that what she could not, none of those that we dreaded could. Though there might be danger to her body, yet her soul was safe!

Presently the horses began to scream, and tore at their tethers till I came to them and quieted them. When they did feel my hands on them, they whinnied low as in joy, and licked at my hands and were quiet for a time. Many times through the night did I come to them, till it arrive to the cold hour when all nature is at lowest; and every time my coming was with quiet of them.

In the cold hour the fire began to die, and now the snow came in flying sweeps and with it a chill mist. Even in the dark there was a light of some kind, as there ever is over snow; and it seemed as though the snow-flurries and the wreaths of mist took shape as of women with trailing garments.

It was as though my memories of all Jonathan's horrid experience were befooling me; for the snowflakes and the mist began to wheel and circle round, till I could get as though a shadowy glimpse of those women that would have kissed him. And then the horses cowered lower and lower, and moaned in terror as men do in pain.

I feared for my dear Madam Mina when these weird figures drew near and circled round. I looked at her, but she sat calm, and smiled at me; when I would have stepped to the fire to replenish it, she caught me and held me back, and whispered, like a voice that one hears in a dream, so low it was, "No! No! Do not go without. Here you are safe!"

I turned to her, and looking in her eyes, said, "But you? It is for you that I fear!"

Whereat she laughed – a laugh low and unreal – and said, "Fear for *me*! Why fear for me? None safer in all the world from them than I am," and as I wondered at the meaning of her words, a puff of wind made the flame leap up, and I see the red scar on her forehead. Then, alas! I knew.

Did I not, I would soon have learned, for the wheeling figures of mist and snow came closer, but keeping ever without the Holy circle. Then they began to materialize, till – if God have not take away my reason, for I saw it through my eyes – there were before me in actual flesh the same three women that Jonathan saw in the room, when they would have kissed his throat. I knew the swaying round forms, the bright hard eyes, the white teeth, the ruddy colour, the voluptuous lips.

They smiled at poor dear Madam Mina; and as their laugh came through the silence of the night, they twined their arms and pointed to her, and said in so sweet tingling tones, "Come, sister. Come to us. Come! Come!"

In fear I turned to my poor Madam Mina, and my heart with gladness leapt like flame; for oh! the terror in her sweet eyes, the repulsion, the horror, told a story to my heart that was all of hope. God be thanked she was not, yet, of them.

I seized some of the firewood which was by me, and holding out some of the Wafer, advanced on them towards the fire. They drew back before me, and laughed their low horrid laugh. I fed the fire, and feared them not; for I knew that we were safe within our protections. They could not approach me, whilst so armed, nor Madam Mina whilst she remained within the ring, which she could not leave no more than they could enter. The horses had ceased to moan, and lay still on the ground; the snow fell on them softly, and they grew whiter. I knew that there was for the poor beasts no more of terror.

And so we remained till the red of the dawn began to fall through the snow-gloom. I was desolate and afraid, and full of woe and terror; but when that beautiful sun began to climb the horizon life was to me again. At the first coming of the dawn the horrid figures melted in the whirling mist and snow; the wreaths of transparent gloom moved away towards the castle, and were lost.

Instinctively, with the dawn coming, I turned to Madam Mina, intending to hypnotize her; but she lay in a deep and sudden sleep, from which I could not wake her. I tried to hypnotize through her sleep, but she made no response, none at all; and the day broke.

I fear yet to stir. I have made my fire and have seen the horses; they are all dead. Today I have much to do here, and I keep waiting till the sun is up high; for there may be places where I must go, where that sunlight, though snow and mist obscure it, will be to me a safety.

I will strengthen me with breakfast, and then I will to my terrible work. Madam Mina still sleeps; and, God be thanked, she is calm in her sleep...

*On the same dawn, Dr Seward and Quincey Morris watched with mixed feelings as the leiter-wagon transporting the Un-Dead body of Count Dracula dashed away, surrounded by its Szgany escort, from the vessel that had brought it up the river. The box had landed safely on the bank, with only one, short, journey to make before it reached the castle. They had heard along the way that Jonathan and Godalming had been wrecked, but had no idea at all if they had managed to get much further on – or where, indeed, they were.*

*Seward's note mixes optimism with despair:* The snow is falling lightly and there is a strange excitement in the air. It may be our own excited feelings, but the depression is strange. Far off I hear the howling of wolves; the snow brings them down from the mountains, and there are dangers to all of us, and from all sides. The horses are nearly ready, and we are soon off. We ride to death of someone. God alone knows who, or where, or what, or when, or how it may be...

# 6

# Inside the Castle

*Memorandum by Abraham Van Helsing*

*5 November, afternoon* – I am sane. Thank God for that mercy
at all events, though the proving it has been dreadful.

When I left Madam Mina sleeping within the Holy circle, I took my way to the castle. The blacksmith hammer which I took in the carriage from Veresti was useful; though the doors were all open I broke them off the rusty hinges, lest some ill-intent or ill-chance should close them, so that being entered I might not get out. Jonathan's bitter experience served me here.

By memory of his diary I found my way to the old chapel, for I knew that here my work lay. The air was oppressive; it seemed as if there was some sulphurous fume, which at times made me dizzy. Either there was a roaring in my ears or I heard afar off the howl of wolves.

I knew that there were at least three graves to find – graves that are inhabit; so I search, and search, and I find one of them.

She lay in her Vampire sleep, so full of life and voluptuous beauty that I shudder as though I have come to do murder. I doubt not that in old time, when such things were, many a man who set forth to do such a task as mine found at the last his heart fail him. So he delay, and delay, and delay, till the mere beauty and the fascination hypnotize him till the Vampire sleep be over. Then the beautiful eyes of the fair woman open and look love, and the voluptuous mouth present to a kiss – and man is weak. Yes, I was moved. I, Van Helsing, with all my purpose and with my motive for hate – I was moved to a yearning for delay which seemed to paralyse my faculties and to clog my very soul.

I was lapsing into sleep, the open-eyed sleep of one who yields, when there came through the snow-stilled air a long, low wail, so full of woe and pity that it woke me like the sound of a clarion. It was the voice of my dear Madam Mina.

Then I braced myself again to my horrid task, and found by wrenching away tomb-tops one other of the sisters, the other dark one. I dared not pause to look on her, lest once more I should begin to be enthrall; but I go on searching until, presently, I find that other fair sister which, like Jonathan, I had seen to gather herself out of the atoms of the mist.

She was so fair to look on, so radiantly beautiful, so exquisitely voluptuous, that the very instinct of man in me, which calls some of my sex to love and to protect one of hers, made my head whirl with new emotion. But, God be thanked, that soul-wail of my dear Madam Mina had not died out of my ears; and, before the spell could be wrought further upon me, I had nerved myself to my wild work.

By this time I had searched all the chapel, so far as I could tell; and there was one great tomb more lordly than the rest; huge it was, and nobly proportioned. On it was but one word:

# DRACULA

This then was the Un-Dead home of the King-Vampire. Its emptiness spoke eloquent. Before I began to restore these women to their dead selves through my awful work, I laid in Dracula's tomb some of the Wafer, and so banished him from it, Un-Dead, for ever.

Then began my terrible task, and I dreaded it. Had it been but one, it had been easy, comparative. But three! To begin twice more after I had been through a deed of horror; for if it was terrible with the sweet Miss Lucy, what would it not be with these strange ones who had survived through centuries, and who had been strengthened by the passing of the years; who would, if they could, have fought for their foul lives...

Oh, my friend John, but it was butcher work; had I not been nerved by thoughts of other dead, and of the living over whom hung such a pall of fear, I could not have gone on. I tremble and tremble even yet, though till all was over, God be thanked, my nerve did stand.

Had I not seen the repose in the first face, and the gladness that stole over it, I could not have gone further with my butchery. I could not have endured the horrid screeching as the stake drove home; the plunging of writhing form, and lips of bloody foam. I should have fled in terror and left my work undone.

But it is over! And the poor souls, I can pity them now and weep, as I think of them placid each in her full sleep of death, for a short moment ere fading. For, friend John, hardly had my knife severed the head of each, before the whole body began to melt away and crumble into its native dust, as though the death that should have come centuries agone had at last assert himself and say at once and loud, "I am here!"

Before I left the castle I so fixed its entrances that never more can the Count enter there Un-Dead.

When I stepped into the circle where Madam Mina slept, she woke from her sleep, and, seeing me, cried out in pain that I had endured too much.

"Come!" she said. "Come away from this awful place! Let us go to meet my husband, who is, I know, coming towards us." She was looking thin and pale and weak; but her eyes were pure and glowed with fervour. I was glad to see her paleness and her illness, for my mind was full of the fresh horror of that ruddy vampire sleep.

And so with trust and hope, and yet full of fear, we go eastward to meet our friends - and *him* - whom Madam Mina tell me that she *know* are coming to meet us.

# *Life ... and Death*

*Van Helsing could do nothing to shake Mina Harker's conviction that her husband and their friends were travelling towards them. And even if it were not true, they had no alternative but to go and meet the returning Dracula head on – and trust in God that they could still defeat him. It was left to Mina to relate in her journal the final moments of their appalling struggle.*

## *Mina Harker's Journal*

6 November – It was late in the afternoon when the Professor and I took our way towards the east whence I knew Jonathan

was coming. We did not go fast, though the way was steeply downhill, for we had to take heavy rugs and wraps with us; we dared not face the possibility of being left without warmth in the cold and the snow. We had to take some of our provisions too, for we were in a perfect desolation, and, so far as we could see through the snowfall, there was not even the sign of habitation.

When we had gone about a mile, I was tired with the heavy walking and sat down to rest. Then we looked back and saw where the clear line of Dracula's castle cut the sky in all its grandeur.

Perched a thousand feet on the summit of a sheer precipice, and with seemingly a great gap between it and the steep of the adjacent mountain on any side, there was something wild and uncanny about the place. We could hear the distant howling of wolves.

I knew from the way Dr Van Helsing was searching about that he was trying to seek some strategic point, where we would be less exposed in case of attack. The rough roadway still led downwards; we could trace it through the drifted snow.

In a little while the Professor signalled to me, so I got up and joined him. He had found a wonderful spot, a sort of natural hollow in a rock, with an entrance like a doorway between two boulders. He took me by the hand and drew me in.

"See!" he said. "Here you will be in shelter; and if the wolves do come I can meet them one by one."

He brought in our furs, and made a snug nest for me, and got out some provisions and forced them upon me. But I could not eat; to even try to do so was repulsive to me, and, much as I would have liked to please him, I could not bring myself to the attempt. He looked very sad, but did not reproach me. Taking his field glasses from the case, he stood on the top of the rock, and began to search the horizon.

Suddenly he called out, "Look! Madam Mina, look! Look!"

I sprang up and stood beside him on the rock; he handed me his glasses and pointed. The snow was now falling more heavily, and swirled about fiercely, for a high wind was beginning to blow. However, there were times when there were pauses between the snow flurries and I could see a long way round.

Straight in front of us and not far off – in fact so near that I wondered we had not noticed before – came a group of mounted men hurrying along. In the midst of them was a cart, a long leiter-wagon which swept from side to side, like a dog's tail wagging, with each stern inequality of the road. Outlined against the snow as they were, I could see from the men's clothes that they were peasants or gypsies of some kind.

On the cart was a great square chest. My heart leaped as I saw it, for I felt that the end was coming. The evening was now drawing close, and well I knew that at sunset the Thing, which was till then imprisoned there, would take new freedom and could in any of many forms elude all pursuit. In fear I turned to the Professor; to my consternation, however, he was not there. An instant later, I saw him below me. Round the rock he had drawn a circle, such as we had found shelter in last night.

When he had completed it he stood beside me again, saying, "At least you shall be safe here from *him!*" He took the glasses from me, and at the next lull of the snow swept the whole space below us. "See," he said, "they come quickly; they are flogging the horses, and galloping as hard as they can."

He paused and went on in a hollow voice, "They are racing for the sunset. We may be too late. God's will be done!" Down came another blinding rush of driving snow, and the whole landscape was blotted out. It soon passed, however, and once more his glasses were fixed on the plain.

Then came a sudden cry: "Look! Look! Look! See, two horsemen follow fast, coming up from the south. It must be Quincey and John. Take the glass. Look, before the snow blots it all out!" I took it and looked. The two men might be Dr Seward and Mr Morris. I knew at all events that neither of them was Jonathan.

At the same time I *knew* that Jonathan was not far off; looking around I saw on the north side of the coming party two other men, riding at breakneck speed. One of them I knew was Jonathan, and the other I took, of course, to be Lord Godalming. They, too, were pursuing the party with the cart.

When I told the Professor he shouted in glee like a schoolboy, and, after looking intently till a snowfall made sight impossible, he laid his Winchester rifle ready for use against the boulder at the opening of our shelter.

"They are all converging," he said. "When the time comes we shall have the gypsies on all sides." I got out my revolver ready to hand, for whilst we were speaking the howling of wolves came louder and closer.

When the snowstorm abated a moment we looked again. It was strange to see the snow falling in such heavy flakes close to us, and beyond, the sun shining more and more brightly as it sank down towards the far mountain tops. Sweeping the glass all around us I could see here and there dots moving singly and in twos and threes and larger numbers - the wolves were gathering for their prey.

Every instant seemed an age whilst we waited. The wind came now in fierce bursts, and the snow was driven with fury as it swept upon us in circling eddies. At times we could not see an arm's length before us; but at others as the hollow-sounding wind swept by us, it seemed to clear the air space so that we could see afar. We had of late been so accustomed to watch for sunrise and sunset, that we knew with fair accuracy when it would be; and we knew that before long the sun would set.

It was hard to believe that by our watches it was less than an hour that we waited in that rocky shelter before the various bodies began to converge close upon us. The wind came now with fiercer and more bitter sweeps, and more steadily from the north. It seemingly had driven the snow clouds from us, for we could distinguish clearly the individuals of each party, the pursued and the pursuers. They seemed to hasten with redoubled speed as the sun dropped lower and lower on the mountain tops.

Closer and closer they drew. The Professor and I crouched

down behind our rock, and held our weapons ready; I could see that he was determined that they should not pass. One and all were quite unaware of our presence.

All at once two voices shouted out: "Halt!" One was my Jonathan's, raised in a high key of passion; the other, Mr Morris's strong resolute tone of quiet command. The gypsies may not have known the language, but there was no mistaking the tone, in whatever tongue the words were spoken. Instinctively they reined in, and at the instant Lord Godalming and Jonathan dashed up at one side and Dr Seward and Mr Morris on the other.

The leader of the gypsies, a splendid-looking fellow who sat his horse like a centaur, waved them back, and in a fierce voice gave to his companions some word to proceed. They lashed the horses, which sprang forward; but the four men raised their Winchester rifles, and in an unmistakable way commanded them to stop. At the same moment Dr Van Helsing and I rose behind the rock and pointed our weapons at them.

Seeing that they were surrounded the men tightened their reins and drew up. The leader turned to them and gave a word at which every man of the gypsy party drew what weapon he carried, knife or pistol, and held himself in readiness to attack. Issue was joined in an instant.

The leader, with a quick movement of his rein, threw his horse out in front, and pointing first to the sun – now close down on the hilltops - and then to the castle, said something which I did not understand. For answer, all four men of our party threw themselves from their horses and dashed towards the cart. I should have felt terrible fear at seeing Jonathan in such danger, but that the ardour of battle must have been upon me; I felt only a wild, surging desire to do something.

Seeing the quick movement of our parties, the leader of the gypsies gave a command; his men instantly formed round the cart in a sort of undisciplined endeavour, each one shouldering and pushing the other in his eagerness to carry out the order.

In the midst of this I could see that Jonathan on one side of the ring of men, and Quincey on the other, were forcing a way to the cart; they were bent on finishing their task before the sun should set. Nothing seemed to stop or even to hinder them. Neither the levelled weapons or the flashing knives of the gypsies in front, or the howling of the wolves behind, appeared to even attract their attention.

Jonathan's impetuosity, and the manifest singleness of his purpose, seemed to overawe those in front of him; instinctively they cowered aside and let him pass. In an instant he had jumped upon the cart, and, with a strength which seemed incredible, raised the great box, and flung it to the ground.

In the meantime, Mr Morris had had to use force to pass through his side of the ring of Szgany. All the time I had been breathlessly watching Jonathan I had, with the tail of my eye, seen him pressing desperately forward, and had seen the knives of the gypsies flash as he won a way through them, and they cut at him. He had parried with his great bowie knife, and at first I thought that he too had come through in safety; but as he sprang beside Jonathan, who had by now jumped from the cart, I could see that with his left hand he was clutching at his side, and that the blood was spurting through his fingers.

He did not delay notwithstanding this, for as Jonathan, with desperate energy, attacked one end of the chest, attempting to prize off the lid with his great Kukri knife, he attacked the other frantically with his bowie. Under the efforts of both men the lid began to yield; the nails drew with a quick screeching sound, and the top of the box was thrown back.

By this time the gypsies, seeing themselves covered by the Winchesters, and at the mercy of Lord Godalming and Dr Seward, had given in and made no further resistance. The sun was almost down on the mountain tops, and the shadows of the whole group fell upon the snow. I saw the Count lying within the box upon the earth, some of which the rude falling from the cart had scattered over him. He was deathly pale, just like a waxen image, and the red eyes glared with the horrible vindictive look which I knew so well.

As I looked, the eyes saw the sinking sun, and the look of hate in them turned to triumph.

But, on the instant, came the sweep and flash of Jonathan's great knife. I shrieked as I saw it shear through the throat; whilst at the same moment Mr Morris's bowie knife plunged into the heart.

It was like a miracle; but before our very eyes, and almost in the drawing of a breath, the whole body crumbled into dust and passed from our sight. I shall be glad as long as I live that even in that moment of final dissolution, there was in the face a look of peace, such as I never could have imagined might have rested there.

The Castle of Dracula now stood out against the red sky, and every stone of its broken battlements was articulated against the light of the setting sun.

The gypsies, taking us as in some way the cause of the extraordinary disappearance of the dead man, turned, without a word, and rode away as if for their lives. Those who were unmounted jumped upon the leiter-wagon and shouted to the horsemen not to desert them. The wolves, which had withdrawn to a safe distance, followed in their wake, leaving us alone.

Mr Morris, who had sunk to the ground, leaned on his elbow, his hand pressed to his side; the blood still gushed through his fingers. I flew to him, for the Holy circle did not now keep me back; so did the two doctors. Jonathan knelt behind him and the wounded man laid back his head on his shoulder. With a sigh, he took my hand in that of his own which was unstained.

He must have seen the anguish of my heart in my face, for he smiled at me and said, "I am only too happy to have been of any service!

"Oh, God!" he cried suddenly, struggling up to a sitting posture and pointing to me. "It was worth this to die! Look! Look!"

The sun was now right down upon the mountain top, and the red gleams fell upon my face, so that it was bathed in rosy light. With one impulse the men sank on their knees and a deep and earnest "Amen" broke from all as their eyes followed the pointing of his finger as the dying man spoke.

"Now God be thanked that all has not been in vain! See! The snow is not more stainless than her forehead! The curse has passed away!"

And, to our bitter grief, with a smile and in silence, he died, a gallant gentleman.

# The Aftermath

## A Note

Seven years ago we all went through the flames; and the happiness of some of us since then is, we think, well worth the pain we endured. It is an added joy to Mina and to me that our boy's birthday is the same day as that on which Quincey Morris died. His mother holds, I know, the secret belief that some of our brave friend's spirit has passed into him. His bundle of names links all our little band of men together; but we call him Quincey.

In the summer of this year we made a journey to Transylvania, and went over the old ground which was, and is, to us so full of vivid and terrible memories. It was almost impossible to believe that the things which we had seen with our own eyes and heard with our own ears were living truths. Every trace of all that had been was blotted out. The castle stood as before, reared high above a waste of desolation.

When we got home we were talking of the old time – which we could all look back on without despair, for Godalming and Seward are both happily married. I took the papers from the safe where they had been ever since our return so long ago.

We were struck with the fact, that in all the mass of material of which the record is composed, there is hardly one authentic document; nothing but a mass of typewriting, except the later notebooks of Mina and Seward and myself, and Van Helsing's memorandum. We could hardly ask anyone, even did we wish to, to accept these as proofs of so wild a story.

Van Helsing summed it all up as he said, with our boy on his knee, "We want no proofs; we ask none to believe us! This boy will some day know what a brave and gallant woman his mother is. Already he knows her sweetness and loving care; later on he will understand how some men so loved her, that they did dare much for her sake."

*Jonathan Harker*

*Dracula* was first published in 1897 by Archibald Constable and Company

This edition first published 2004 by Walker Books Ltd
87 Vauxhall Walk, London SE11 5HJ

2 4 6 8 10 9 7 5 3 1

This abridged version © 2004 Jan Needle
Illustrations © 2004 Gary Blythe

The right of Jan Needle and Gary Blythe to be identified as
author and illustrator respectively of this work has been asserted by
them in accordance with the Copyright, Designs and Patents Act 1988

This book has been typeset in BarbedorT and Aqualine

Printed in China

British Library Cataloguing in Publication Data:
a catalogue record for this book is available
from the British Library

ISBN 0-7445-8653-4

www.walkerbooks.co.uk